MIDNIGHT SONS

DEBBIE MACOMBER

Falling For Him

Harlequin Books

TORONTO • NEW YORK • LONDON
AMSTERDAM • PARIS • SYDNEY • HAMBURG
STOCKHOLM • ATHENS • TOKYO • MILAN
MADRID • WARSAW • BUDAPEST • AUCKLAND

ISBN 0-373-03399-0

FALLING FOR HIM

First North American Publication 1996.

Copyright © 1996 by Debbie Macomber.

This edition published by arrangement with Harlequin Books S.A.

® and TM are trademarks of the publisher. Trademarks indicated with ® are registered in the United States Patent and Trademark Office, the Canadian Trade Marks Office and in other countries.

Printed in U.S.A.

The History of Hard Luck, Alaska

Hard Luck, situated fifty miles north of the Arctic Circle, near the Brooks Mountain Range, was founded by Adam O'Halloran and his wife, Anna, in 1931. Adam came to Alaska to make his fortune, but never found the gold strike he sought. Nevertheless, the O'Hallorans and their two young sons, Charles and David, stayed on—in part because of a tragedy that befell the family a few years later.

Other prospectors and adventurers began to move to Hard Luck, some of them bringing wives and children. The town became a stopping-off place for mail, equipment and supplies. The Fletcher family arrived in 1938 to open a dry goods store.

When World War II began, Hard Luck's population was fifty or sixty people, all told. Some of the younger men, including the O'Halloran sons, joined the armed services; Charles left for Europe in 1942, David in 1944 at the age of eighteen. Charles died during the fighting. Only David came home—with a young English war bride, Ellen Sawyer (despite the fact that he'd become engaged to Catherine Fletcher shortly before going overseas).

After the war, David qualified as a bush pilot. He then built some small cabins to attract the sport fishermen and hunters who were starting to come to Alaska; he also worked as a guide. Eventually, in the early seventies, he built a lodge to replace the cabins— a lodge that later burned.

David and Ellen had three sons, born fairly late in their marriage—Charles (named after David's brother) was born in 1960, Sawyer in 1963 and Christian in 1965.

Hard Luck had been growing slowly all this time, and by 1970 it was home to just over a hundred people. These were the years of the oil boom, when the school and community center were built by the state. After Vietnam, ex-serviceman Ben Hamilton joined the community and opened the Hard Luck Café, which became the social focus for the town.

In the late 1980s, the three O'Halloran brothers formed a partnership, creating Midnight Sons, a bush-pilot service. They were awarded the mail contract, and also delivered fuel and other necessities to the interior. In addition, they serve as a small commuter airline, flying passengers to and from Fairbanks and within the North Arctic.

At the time these stories start, there are approximately 150 people living in Hard Luck—a preponderance of them male....

Dear Reader,

Welcome to the town of Hard Luck, Alaska! I hope you'll join me there to meet the Midnight Sons, their families, friends and wives-to-be.

The people I want to credit with the idea for this project are, in fact, fictional—they're Valerie, Stephanie and Norah, the three sisters I wrote about in the Orchard Valley trilogy (Harlequin Romances #3232, 3239, 3244). I loved writing those books, I loved the characters and the town and last but definitely not least, I loved the way readers responded to the stories.

So when Harlequin suggested this six-book project, I was thrilled. Soon after that, the town of Hard Luck, the O'Halloran brothers and Midnight Sons all came to life. Never have I worked harder on a project, nor have I enjoyed my research more. In the summer of 1994, my husband and I traveled to Alaska, and I fell in love with the state—its sheer magnificence, the warmth of its people, the excitement of life on the "last frontier."

Now I invite you to sit back, put your feet up and allow me to introduce you to some proud, stubborn, *wonderful* men—Alaskan men—and show you what happens when they meet their real matches. Women from the "lower forty-eight." Women with the courage to change their lives and take risks for love. Women a lot like you and me!

Love,

Debbie

Debbie Macomber is one of the most popular romance authors writing today. She's written more than seventy romances (for Harlequin and Silhouette) and several bestselling "mainstream" women's fiction novels. Not surprisingly, Debbie has won a number of awards for her books.

She lives in Washington State with her husband, Wayne, and their dog, Peterkins. They have four grown children—and they've just become grandparents! Debbie's *thrilled* with her new granddaughter, Jazmine Lynn.

Debbie loves to hear from her readers. You can reach her at: P.O. Box 1458, Port Orchard, Washington 98366.

Books by Debbie Macomber

CHAPTER ONE

THE WOMAN DROVE him crazy. Christian O'Halloran had given a *lot* of thought to Mariah Douglas lately and had compiled a long list of reasons to fire her. Good reasons. Unfortunately he had yet to get his stubborn brother to agree. According to Sawyer, Mariah could do no wrong.

According to him, she could do no right.

It astonished Christian that his brother was so blind about this. As a rule, Christian valued Sawyer's opinion. In fact, he considered both his older brothers—Charles, too—excellent judges of character. Christian couldn't understand it, but they'd been hoodwinked by Mariah. Not only that, they'd accused *him* of being arbitrary, unfair, unkind.

Mariah gave the impression of being sweet and gentle-natured. Unassuming. Incredibly efficient. But he knew otherwise, Christian thought darkly. Mariah Douglas was not to be trusted. She was, to put it simply, a klutz. Whenever he was around, she lost messages, misfiled documents, dropped things. None of that ever seemed to happen when Sawyer was in the office, so Christian had to conclude that she had it in for him, and him alone. Now, he didn't believe she'd ever *intentionally* do anything to undermine their business. If she managed to sabotage Midnight Sons, he was convinced it would be purely accidental. That, however, didn't make her any less dangerous. There was definitely a negative chemistry between them. He nodded to himself, pleased with the term.

Sitting at his desk in the mobile office for Midnight Sons, the flight service the three O'Halloran brothers owned and operated in Hard Luck, Alaska, Christian wondered exactly what it was about Mariah he found so objectionable—aside from her clumsiness, of course. He'd never really figured that out.

It wasn't her looks. The woman was attractive enough—medium height, medium build with medium-length red hair and brown eyes. Some might even think she was pretty, and Christian wouldn't disagree. She *was* pretty. Sort of. Nothing that would stop traffic, mind you, but reasonably pleasing to the eye.

Duke Porter, one of his pilots, apparently thought so.

Christian's mouth thinned at the memory of walking in on them recently and finding Mariah and Duke locked in each other's arms. It irritated him no end that those two hadn't kept their romance out of the office. If they wanted to smooch and carry on, they could do it on their own time. Not his.

This sort of behavior wasn't what he'd had in mind when he convinced Sawyer that they should bring women to Hard Luck. In his view, the plan had a practical business purpose. Midnight Sons had been losing pilots. And he'd hoped that convincing women to move to Alaska would solve their problems.

Instead, it had created more. Mariah Douglas being one of them.

Abbey Sutherland had been the first woman to arrive. From the moment his levelheaded brother laid eyes on her, Sawyer had never been the same. In less than a month, he and Abbey were engaged.

In Christian's opinion, Sawyer lost more than his heart when he met Abbey; since then, his brain hadn't functioned properly, either. Charles wasn't much better once Lanni Caldwell arrived. The two of *them* were engaged by the end of the summer. The newlyweds had set up house this past April, and all the common sense Charles used to have had flown right out the proverbial window.

Christian appeared to be the last of the three in full possession of his wits.

Shortly after he'd found Mariah and Duke embracing, Christian had approached Charles. He'd hoped his oldest brother would help him convince Sawyer that the time had come to replace Mariah. She'd been their secretary for a full year now, and there was only so much a man should have to take. They'd signed a one-year agreement, and as far as he was concerned their responsibilities toward her had been met.

Charles had proved to be a major disappointment. It wasn't that his brother had sided with Sawyer over the secretary issue; he hadn't said what Christian wanted to hear. Charles seemed to feel that Sawyer and Christian should settle this matter between themselves.

That would never work, because Sawyer didn't have the same difficulties with Mariah that Christian did. His brother was in favor of keeping her as long as she wanted to stay on.

Every time Christian brought up the subject, Sawyer reminded him that *he'd* been the one to hire her. What his brother failed to remember was that Christian had never intended Mariah to be their secretary in the first place. He'd wanted Allison Reynolds.

Even now, the image of the tall, beautiful blonde stirred his blood. He'd met her in Seattle and been immediately captivated. It had taken a lot of fancy foot-work to convince her to give Hard Luck a try.

Allison had come, but after viewing the town and seeing the living quarters allotted her, she'd experienced a sudden change of heart. Unfortunately Christian hadn't been in Hard Luck at the time, and once she'd decided to return to Seattle, he didn't have the chance to talk her into giving the town a try.

Disheartened after her departure, he'd pulled out another job application, the first one in the pile.

Mariah Douglas.

Christian had rued that day ever since. He'd wanted Allison Reynolds. She'd affected him the way Abbey had affected Sawyer, the way Lanni affected Charles. If he hadn't been so dismayed with Allison's decision to go back home, he'd have done a better job of choosing her replacement.

"Christian, could I speak to you a moment?" Mariah approached his desk in her usual timid manner, as though she expected him to leap up and bite her.

He raised his eyes until they met hers. It had taken her the better part of six months to call him by his first name, instead of Mr. O'Halloran. Didn't she realize he and Sawyer had the same surname? He sighed. And Sawyer wasn't even in today to help with damage control; he'd gone to Fairbanks with Abbey and the kids.

"Yes," he muttered, barely hiding his impatience.

"Before he left, Sawyer said I should talk to you..." She bit her lower lip. From her expression, you'd think he was some kind of ogre. Christian saw himself as considerate and intelligent and hoped he behaved that way. Obviously Mariah didn't think so. He sighed again.

"Talk to me about what?" he asked, more kindly this time.

"I've been with Midnight Sons a full year now."

No one was more aware of that than Christian. "Yes, I know."

"I'd like to take a week of the vacation allowed me in my employment package."

Christian straightened. A week without Mariah. A week of freedom. A week of peace.

"I'm meeting a friend in Anchorage," she explained, not that he needed to know or particularly cared.

"When?" The sooner she left the better, as far as Christian was concerned. This would be his chance to prove to Sawyer once and for all that they didn't need a secretary. Or—and this was his own preference—that they should hire someone else. Someone more like Allison and a whole lot less like Mariah.

"If it's possible, I'd like to take next week," she said, her eyes hopeful. "Early August is a perfect time of year to see Alaska."

"Next week'll be fine." Christian was so excited it was all he could do not to grip her by the shoulders and kiss her on both cheeks.

She hesitated, lingering at his desk.

"Is there something else?" he asked.

"Yes, there is." Her eyes flashed briefly, but with what he couldn't quite guess. Anxiety? Resentment? "I wanted to thank you for giving me this time off on such short notice. I realize it puts you in a bind, but I didn't decide to go until last night after Tracy's letter arrived and—"

"Tracy Santiago?"

Mariah nodded.

Tracy was an attorney hired by the Douglas family soon after Mariah's arrival. Tracy had flown up to inspect the living conditions and review Mariah's contract with Midnight Sons. Apparently, through all of this, Mariah and Tracy had struck up a friendship.

With any luck Tracy would convince Mariah to give up Alaska and return to Seattle where she belonged. One thing was certain: Christian wanted her gone.

"I'll be leaving on Saturday," she said, again giving him more information than he wanted or required.

"Fine."

"And be back the following Saturday."

"Fine."

She backed away from him. "I just thought you should know."

"Will you be flying out of Fairbanks?"

"Yes." She nodded enthusiastically. "Duke's agreed to take me into the city."

Duke. Christian should have known he'd relish a chance to spend time alone with Mariah. Duke was welcome to her, although Christian would insist they keep their romance out of the office and out of his sight. The problems of having one of his pilots involved with the secretary were obvious—weren't they? Well, maybe he couldn't articulate all the problems this very minute, but he knew instinctively that it wasn't a good idea. For reasons he couldn't entirely explain, Christian did not want Duke flying Mariah into Fairbanks.

"Duke's going to be busy next Saturday," Christian announced suddenly. He wasn't sure what he'd assign the pilot, but he'd come up with something.

"But I checked the schedule, and there wasn't anything down for Duke. He's already said he'd do it, and—"

"Then I suggest you check the schedule again," he snapped, "and have one of the other pilots fly you in."

"All right." She agreed readily enough, but Christian could see she wasn't pleased.

He'd no sooner resumed his paperwork than Mariah approached him a second time.

"Yes?" he said, realizing he sounded annoyed and unable to help it. Then he reminded himself—in a few days he'd be free of her for an entire week. The thought cheered him considerably.

"I've gone over the list, and there's only one other pilot available this Saturday but—"

"Fine." Christian didn't care who flew her into Fairbanks, as long as it wasn't Duke.

"But—"

He clenched his jaw, growing impatient. "Mariah, I have more important things to do than discuss your travel arrangements. Someone other than Duke will be available to fly you out in plenty of time to catch your flight to Anchorage, and that's all that matters."

"Yes, I know," she returned, just as impatient. "That someone is *you*."

THE MAN WAS IMPOSSIBLE, Mariah decided as she left the Midnight Sons office that afternoon. Nothing she did pleased him. What she should have done was look Christian O'Halloran right in the eye and tell him he could take this job and shove it.

She would've, too, if she wasn't so damned much in love with him.

Mariah didn't know when it had happened, possibly the first time they'd met. He'd been in Seattle interviewing applicants for a variety of positions in Hard Luck. She'd been excited about applying for the job, although as claims adjuster for a large insurance company, she had limited office experience.

Her meeting with Christian had been short and to the point. He'd asked her a list of questions, but his mind seemed to be elsewhere. She left, discouraged, convinced he'd already made his decision and wouldn't be giving her the job.

When she learned she *had* gotten the job and told her friends, no one seemed to understand her reasons for wanting to move to a remote town north of the Arctic Circle. If she was doing it to escape her family, they told her, there were any number of places that would have been more suitable.

Her friends' doubts were nothing compared to her family's reaction. When she'd informed her parents that she planned to move to Hard Luck, they'd feared the worst.

She couldn't make them understand that Alaska appealed to her sense of adventure, her need to experience a different life. She'd suspected she would grow to love this land, and she'd been right.

Her friends had teased her unmercifully. She still grinned whenever she remembered a comment of her friend Rochelle's: "I hear your odds of finding a man are good—but the goods are odd."

Mariah hadn't come to Alaska looking for a husband. No one seemed to understand that. She'd come because she wanted a life of her own, a life away from her family. She wanted to make her own decisions and her own mistakes. For the first time, she didn't have her mother or one of her aunts looking over her shoulder, ready to leap into the middle of her life and arrange everything.

Two important occurrences had shaped her year in Hard Luck. First and foremost, she'd fallen in love.

Head over heels. Hook, line and sinker. The whole nine yards.

The problem was that the object of her affections was Christian O'Halloran and he didn't even seem to *like* her. He thought she was a major klutz, and in the past year she'd done everything possible to prove him right. Not intentionally of course. The man flustered her terribly. Every time they were in close proximity, she said or did something stupid. She couldn't seem to help it. And now he seemed to think she was infatuated with Duke. The man had to be blind.

The second occurrence had been set in motion by her family. Mariah should've realized they'd have a difficult time accepting her decision to move away. The ink had barely dried on her contract with Midnight Sons when her parents had hired an attorney.

Tracy Santiago had turned out to be a blessing in disguise. At first Mariah was afraid the woman would do something to jeopardize her position with Midnight Sons, but her fears had been groundless.

Soon after Mariah's arrival in Hard Luck, Tracy flew up to meet her, and while she was there she interviewed several of the other women. In the year since then, Mariah and Tracy had become close friends.

They'd kept in touch, with letters and phone calls and the occasional brief visit. In that time, there'd been a number of unexpected events. Marriages. A death. A new enterprise—the revived Hard Luck Lodge. And soon the community would see a spurt in population growth. Abbey O'Halloran was pregnant, as was Karen Caldwell. Both were due around the same time, midwinter.

Tracy had thoroughly enjoyed receiving Mariah's letters, updating her on life and love in Hard Luck. Ro-

mance abounded. The two older O'Halloran brothers
had fallen for women in no time flat. They were both
married now. Pete Livengood, who operated the gen-
eral store, had married Dotty Harlow, the health clinic
nurse, in short order. Then Mitch Harris, the public-
safety officer, and Bethany Ross, the new school-
teacher, had fallen in love. Some women had come and
stayed, others had quickly moved on. Those who did
stay became so integrated in the community it was
sometimes difficult to remember who was new to this
rugged, beautiful place and who wasn't.

Mariah liked writing her long, detailed letters about
the happenings in Hard Luck as much as Tracy liked
reading them. She appreciated Tracy's friendship and
support more than ever.

Mariah's family had been convinced she wouldn't last
six months. But her parents had underestimated her te-
nacity; Tracy hadn't.

Mariah continued walking toward her small cabin. As
she strolled past Hard Luck Lodge, Karen Caldwell
stepped out onto the porch. Karen was four months
pregnant, and radiantly happy.

"Mariah," Karen said, brightening, "I hear you're
going on vacation. That's great news. Where are you
headed?"

This was one thing about living in a small community
that still amazed Mariah. There were few secrets, although people here did seem to respect each other's pri-
vacy. It wasn't as though they were eager to spread
gossip; it was more a matter of genuine interest and
concern. News was passed along in a friendly sort of way
at Ben Hamilton's place. Most everyone in town stopped
in at the Hard Luck Café at least once during the week,
and some more often.

Mariah joined her friend on the front porch of the renovated lodge, which had once belonged to the O'Hallorans and was now owned by Karen's husband, Matt.

"Who told you about my vacation?" she asked, curious to learn how the news had made the rounds.

"Matt. He had coffee with Ben after John Henderson was in this morning."

That explained it. John Henderson was Duke Porter's best friend. She suspected Duke had mentioned he was flying her into Fairbanks, then John had told Ben and Ben had told Matt.

"I'm meeting Tracy Santiago in Anchorage," Mariah explained. "I've been in Alaska over a year now, and I thought it was time I played tourist."

"Have a great time," Karen said. "But don't let the bright lights of the big city dazzle you."

"Not to worry. This is my home." And it was. Mariah had no desire to return to Seattle. Her commitment had been for one year, but she fully expected to settle in Hard Luck permanently. The cabin, for whatever it was worth, and the twenty acres of land promised her in the contract had been fully deeded to her. Mariah had achieved what she'd wanted. Nothing held her in Hard Luck now except her love of the community and those in it.

Especially Christian.

CHRISTIAN WALKED into the Hard Luck Café and slid onto a stool at the counter. Ben Hamilton was busy writing the dinner special on the blackboard. Moose pot roast in cranberry sauce with mashed potatoes and gravy. Christian studied the board intently.

"It's a little early to be eating, isn't it?" Ben asked.

"Of course it is." It was only four-thirty, and he generally didn't have dinner until six or later.

"You just ate lunch three hours ago," Ben reminded him.

Christian knew exactly when he'd had lunch. He hadn't come into the café for food. He wanted to complain. Sawyer had only been gone a day, and already Christian felt at the end of his rope. Between dealing with Mariah and the increased workload, he'd completely lost his patience and his composure. His brother had taken a jaunt into Fairbanks with Abbey and the kids to meet some friends. Christian didn't want to think what would happen if Sawyer stayed away longer than a couple of days.

"You got something on your mind?" Ben asked, leaning against the counter.

"Yeah."

"Well, I'll tell you what I said to young Matt not so long ago. If you want advice, it doesn't come free. Not anymore."

"What the hell are you talking about?"

"Did you come in here to eat or to talk?" Ben asked curtly.

Christian had noticed a difference in Ben's temperament ever since he'd started his frequent-eater program. Apparently he'd decided that from now on, nothing was free. Not even speech. Christian was almost surprised Ben wasn't charging him for sitting on the stool.

"How about some coffee?" Christian muttered.

Ben's mouth formed a slow grin. "Coming up."

Christian righted the mug and Ben promptly filled it. Staring at it reminded him that Mariah had made coffee for him nearly every morning for a year. He couldn't count the number of times he'd told her he liked his coffee black. Some days she added sugar, some days cream, some days both. But he could count on one hand the days she'd gotten it right.

"Something bugging you?" Ben asked.

Christian shook his head. Now that he was here, he didn't feel inclined to share his woes. More than likely, Ben would side with Mariah the way his brothers had.

"If you've got a problem, spit it out," Ben advised.

"You going to charge me?" Christian asked jokingly.

"Nah, I'm just looking to sell a little coffee."

Ben probably sold more coffee than some of those all-night diners in Anchorage, but Christian didn't say so.

"If you've got something on your mind," Ben pressed, "best thing to do is get it out."

"It's nothing."

Ben's laugh was skeptical. "My guess is it involves Mariah."

Christian glared at the older man. "What makes you say that?"

The cook lifted one shoulder in a casual shrug. "Whenever I see you frown, it usually has something to do with her. After all, you've been complaining about Mariah for more than a year."

"Not that it does me any good." Christian said with ill grace. "According to everyone else, the woman walks on water. Is there something wrong with me?" he asked, but he didn't really expect an answer.

"She's a sweetheart, Chris."

"Not to me, she isn't." She might be as wonderful as everyone said, but Christian doubted it. "We just can't seem to get along," he mumbled, hoping Ben could accept that.

"Have you ever stopped to consider why?"

"I have, as a matter of fact," Christian said. "I read an article in one of those airline magazines—oh, it must've been a number of years ago. It was about a man who'd walked from one end of the continental United States to the other. Took him months. People from all over asked him what he'd found the hardest."

Ben frowned. "Are we still talking about Mariah?"

"Yes," Christian insisted. "The writer who was doing the interview suggested the hardest part must've been the heat of the desert or the cold of the mountains."

"Was it?" Ben asked, obviously curious now. He folded his arms and waited for Christian to respond.

"Nope."

"You sure we're still talking about Mariah?" Ben asked again.

Christian ignored the question. "After deep thought, the man gave his answer. The most difficult thing about the long walk had been the sand in his shoes."

"The sand in his shoes?"

"Yup. And that's what's wrong between me and Mariah."

Ben's face broke into a network of lines as he frowned, and Christian suspected he assumed Mariah had been pouring sand in his shoes. "It's the little things about her that drive me nuts," he explained. "The fact that she ruins my coffee every morning. The way she loses things and just . . . irritates me." Christian paused, then said grudgingly, "I'm sure she's a perfectly capable secretary—or would be for someone else. But she hasn't worked out for me."

"Sawyer doesn't seem to have a problem with her." Christian had heard this argument from Ben before; he wasn't surprised to be hearing it now.

The door of the café opened just then, and he glanced over his shoulder and saw Duke. The other man's eyes narrowed as he caught sight of Christian.

"What's this all about?" Duke demanded, waving the note Christian had slipped into his cubicle.

"I'll be flying Mariah into Fairbanks on Saturday," Christian told him calmly. He didn't expect the other man to argue, since he was the boss.

"*I* offered to do it," Duke said.

"I know, but there are other, uh, more important things I need you for."

"Like hell. You're sending me out on a wild-goose chase and you know it. I could make the flight into Barrow any time next week, and all at once you decide I have to do it on Saturday."

Christian wasn't proud of his little subterfuge, but his justification was that he didn't want Duke and Mariah furthering their romance on company time. What they did on their own time was entirely up to them, he told himself righteously. But when it came to Midnight Sons...that was another matter.

"You seem to think I'm sweet on her," Duke suggested angrily.

Christian's hands tightened around the coffee mug. He didn't want to get into this.

"Are you?" Ben wanted to know, his eyes eager.

"No," Duke growled. "I've got a girlfriend in Fairbanks I was planning to see."

"You've got a girlfriend in Fairbanks?" Ben repeated. "Since when?"

"Since now."

Christian wasn't sure he should believe him. "What about the other day when I saw you and Mariah kissing?"

Ben's eyes widened. "You saw Duke and Mariah kissing?"

"Sure as hell did." Every time Christian thought about walking into the office and finding them with their arms wrapped around each other, he felt a fresh wave of fury. "Right in the middle of the day, mind you."

Duke knotted his hands into fists. "I *wasn't* kissing Mariah."

Christian wasn't going to sit there and let one of his own pilots lie to him. "I saw you with my own two eyes!"

Duke shifted his weight from one booted foot to the other. "Since you find it so damned important, I'll tell you again. I *wasn't* kissing Mariah."

Christian glared at the man. This was a bold-faced lie; he knew what he'd seen.

Duke lowered his gaze and muttered, "*She* was kissing *me*."

CHAPTER TWO

ON SATURDAY Mariah was at the airfield well before the allotted time of departure, eager to see Tracy again and make their plans for the week. They'd already decided to take a glacier tour and visit some of the other sights in and around Anchorage.

Fierce, dark clouds puckered the sky, filling the morning with shadows and gloom. Not a promising start to her vacation.

"You ready?" Christian marched past her toward the two-seater Luscom. It was the smallest plane in the Midnight Sons fleet and used the least often.

Mariah picked up her suitcase and hurried after him. "I want you to know how much I appreciate this," she said, holding on to the case with both hands. She didn't understand why Christian had insisted on doing this himself, especially when it was so obvious that he considered it an imposition.

Because of the heavy suitcase, she wasn't able to keep pace with him. Eventually he seemed to realize this. He glanced at her over his shoulder, then, without a word, turned back and took the suitcase from her hands.

"What did you pack in here, anyway? Rocks?"

She didn't bother to answer.

When they reached the plane, Christian helped her inside. He stowed her bag, then joined her in the cockpit. She was surprised by how small and intimate the space really was; their shoulders touched as Christian worked the switches and revved the engine.

Mariah snapped her seat belt in place and gazed anxiously at the threatening sky. She wondered if she should tell Christian she wasn't all that keen on flying. She found small planes especially difficult. Give her a Boeing 767 any day of the week over a tiny, little Luscom.

For the sake of peace, she gritted her teeth and said nothing. No need to hand him further ammunition.

The ever-darkening sky didn't bode well. Mariah noted that Christian was watching it closely. He radioed Fairbanks and wrote down the necessary weather information.

"Is there any chance we'll run into a storm?" she asked once they'd started to taxi down the gravel runway.

She expected him to make light of her concern, but he didn't. "According to the flight controller, we should be able to fly above the worst of it. Don't worry, I'll get you to Fairbanks on time."

Or die trying, Mariah mused darkly. She gritted her teeth again and held on for dear life as the single-engine furiously increased speed. Soon they were roaring down the runway, and at what seemed the last possible second, the plane's nose angled toward the sky and the wheels left the ground.

As soon as they were airborne, Mariah relaxed slightly. The flight would take the better part of an hour, possibly a bit longer, depending on the winds.

Within a few minutes, they were swallowed up by the unfriendly clouds. Mariah couldn't see two feet in front of them, but that might well have been a blessing in disguise.

Trying to relieve her tension, she closed her eyes.

"If you feel yourself getting sick," Christian said, "let me know."

"I'm fine," she assured him.

"Your eyes are closed."

"I know." Her fingers gripped the edge of the seat cushion as she concentrated on breathing evenly.

"Why?"

"Because I don't want to look!" she snapped.

Christian chuckled and seemed to enjoy her discomfort. "I haven't crashed in more than a year," he teased. "But now that you mention it, I'm probably due for a big one."

Suddenly the plane began to pitch first to one side, then the other.

"Don't, *please*," Mariah begged.

"I'm not doing this on purpose," Christian muttered.

Mariah opened her eyes and saw that he actually seemed to be struggling to maintain control. "I'm trying to get us above the clouds. Don't worry, everything's well in hand."

The plane pitched sharply to the right and she swallowed a gasp. Although she'd flown in small planes a number of times since coming to work for Midnight Sons, she remained nervous about the experience—more than ever now, when they were flying directly into a storm.

"Are you all right?" Christian asked a minute later.

"Just fly the plane," she said over the noise of the engine.

"You're pale as a sheet," he said.

"Stop worrying about me."

"Listen," he returned, "I'm not going to be able to fly the plane *and* revive you."

"If I pass out—" she squeezed her eyes shut "—don't worry about me."

The plane heaved. She gasped aloud and covered her face with both hands.

"Mariah," Christian said gently. "Everything will be fine in just a few minutes. Trust me." He patted her arm reassuringly.

Usually when he spoke to her, Christian was impatient or sharp or even angry. Most of the time she wasn't sure what crime she was supposed to have committed. But for reasons she'd probably never understand, today, when she needed it most, he'd chosen to reveal this softer side of himself.

Judging by the feel of the plane, Mariah knew they were increasing altitude. Within minutes they were sure to be above the squall and everything would be fine. Just as he'd promised.

"You can look now," Christian told her.

She splayed her fingers and peeked through. Bright sunlight greeted her, and she sighed deeply, relaxing in her seat. The weather couldn't be more perfect.

They traveled in silence for a while.

"Does your boyfriend know you don't like to fly?" Christian's question startled her.

"My boyfriend?" she asked, genuinely perplexed until she remembered that he'd seen her with Duke.

"I'll have you know lover boy put up quite a stink when I told him he wouldn't be flying you into Fairbanks." The disapproval was back in Christian's voice.

Mariah looked out the side window. "No matter what you think, Duke and I are not involved."

"Yeah, that's what he said, too." The skepticism in his voice was plain.

"It's the truth," she insisted.

"Duke claims *you* kissed *him*."

He appeared to be waiting for her to deny or confirm the statement. "I did—in a manner of speaking."

Christian snorted a laugh. "I'll say. You seem to forget I walked in on the two of you with your lips locked."

"It wasn't like that," Mariah said heatedly. "I'd been on the phone with Tracy—"

"On company time?"

"Yes," she admitted reluctantly. He could dock her pay if he wanted.

"Go on," he encouraged.

"Tracy and Duke don't get along."

Christian laughed again. "That's putting it mildly."

"She, Tracy, thought it would be fun if I kissed Duke and said it was from her, and that's what I did. It was all teasing—a joke."

Christian didn't comment.

"Do you believe me?" she asked. It was important that he do so. They had their differences, but trust was a vital factor in any relationship, whether it was a work relationship or a personal one.

"Yeah," Christian admitted grudgingly, "I guess I do. But you should know something in case you do hold any, uh, tender feelings for Duke. He's got a girlfriend in Fairbanks. And he swore to me he's a one-woman man—one at a time, anyway."

"It doesn't matter to me how many girlfriends Duke's got." Although Mariah was surprised. This was the first she'd heard of Duke being romantically involved with anyone. But then, he was a private person and not inclined to share such things with her.

Just when she'd finally relaxed enough to be comfortable, they approached Fairbanks. As soon as the plane descended into the clouds, Mariah stiffened.

"Hey, you aren't going to tense up on me again, are you?"

"Yes, I am." No point in denying it. She closed her eyes as her fingers reshaped the upholstery.

"Don't worry, we'll be down in no time." He was busy after that, communicating with the tower and manipulating the controls.

True to his word, they touched down in a textbook-perfect landing a few minutes later and taxied to the hangar where Midnight Sons kept a truck.

Neither one of them seemed ready to leave the plane. "That wasn't so bad now, was it?" Christian asked, and his gaze settled on her. All at once the atmosphere was charged with excitement. Never had Mariah been so physically aware of him, and he seemed to be experiencing the same reaction to her.

"You're right. The flight wasn't bad at all," she said, realizing how breathless she sounded. "Thank you," she managed.

She meant to open the door and climb out, but Mariah found that her body refused to function. Suddenly Christian leaned close, so close the distance between their mouths became too slight to measure.

She wasn't sure what to think, what to do. She stopped breathing and was convinced Christian did, too. Gradually he eased forward until his mouth grazed hers. His touch was tender. Light. And all too brief.

The effect was, somehow, more devastating than if they'd engaged in a passionate, openmouthed kiss.

Christian reared back as if she'd slapped him.

Mariah couldn't keep from savoring the exquisite sensation. This was what she'd wanted from the first, what she'd been longing for.

Christian opened the door just then, and a rush of air instantly cooled the interior of the plane.

Mariah didn't wait for him to come around and help her down. She did notice that he couldn't seem to get her luggage out of the plane fast enough.

Once they were inside the truck and headed for the terminal, Christian cleared his throat. "I don't want you to attach any... importance to what happened back there," he said brusquely.

"I...won't."

"I didn't mean to do that. It...well, it just happened."

Regret. He had to go and ruin the most perfect moment of her life with regret.

STUPID, STUPID, stupid. Christian didn't know what in the world had possessed him to kiss Mariah. Four days later, and he couldn't keep from dwelling on their last moments alone in the plane. He didn't know *what* he'd been thinking.

That was the answer, he decided—he hadn't been thinking.

Although he'd analyzed the kiss over and over, he couldn't make sense of it. Not once in the entire year Mariah had been employed by Midnight Sons had the thought of kissing her even entered his mind.

Yet in those awkward moments after they'd landed and taxied off the Fairbanks runway, Christian could think of nothing else. The temptation had become too much for him.

Nothing like complicating his life, he thought. And he had no one to blame but himself. True, he'd made an effort to put it behind them, but only a blind man would've missed the stars in Mariah's eyes.

That was the trouble with women. You kissed them a time or two, and they seemed to think it *meant* something. Well, he wanted one thing clear right now. He was not—repeat, not—interested in Mariah Douglas. He didn't even like the woman. If he could find a legal means of getting her completely out of his life, he'd leap at the opportunity.

"You're looking down in the mouth," Sawyer announced as he walked past Christian's desk to his own.

"I'm fine!" he snapped. The last thing he wanted was for Sawyer to learn about that stupid kiss.

"If I didn't know better, I'd say you missed Mariah."

Christian snickered loudly. "Have you noticed how well everything's gone this week?" he asked. He hoped to convince Sawyer that the office had run like clockwork without her. Maybe, just maybe, Sawyer would see reason and agree to do away with the position.

"It's been hectic," Sawyer argued.

"Well, we've been busier than usual," Christian conceded. "But have you stopped to notice how peaceful it is around here? And how we've had no major problems?"

"No problems," Sawyer agreed.

Perhaps this wasn't going to be as difficult as he'd assumed. "We don't need Mariah."

His brother tossed him a disgusted look. "Don't need Mariah? Sure, we've managed without her, but I have to tell you, this place has been hopping. We're getting more business all the time. If everything's running smoothly, then it's because Mariah oiled the gears before she left. I don't know about you, little brother, but I'm counting the hours until she returns."

Christian cursed under his breath. He was counting the hours himself, but not for the same reasons.

"Don't need Mariah?" Sawyer repeated in the same tone of disbelief he'd used earlier. "Tell that to Abbey and the kids. I've been late for dinner every night this week. I don't like working this hard. I've got a wife and family I'd like to see once in a while."

The phone pealed, and Sawyer glared at Christian, who was concentrating on tallying a row of figures. "Since you've got so much free time on your hands, you can answer that."

Christian scowled and reached for the telephone.

"DUKE'S GOT A GIRLFRIEND?" Tracy Santiago asked Mariah as they sat outside the Kenai Lodge and enjoyed the beautiful sunshine. "You've got to be kidding." Tracy didn't bother to disguise her amazement. "What woman would be able to put up with that chauvinistic character for more than five minutes?"

"I don't know. I'm just repeating what Christian told me. It's funny, though," she said, thinking out loud. "Duke's never mentioned anyone."

Tracy raised her face to the sun and grumbled something Mariah couldn't make out.

"Duke's not so bad."

Tracy straightened and sipped her margarita. "The man's a damned nuisance. Let's change the subject, shall we? He has a bad effect on my blood pressure."

Mariah lay back in the lawn chair. They'd spent four full days sight-seeing. Every minute of every day had been full, and Mariah was exhausted; so was Tracy.

Now was the time to relax. Mariah didn't want to think about Hard Luck—and particularly not about

Christian. This was her vacation, and she was determined to make the most of it.

"Mmm, this is the life," Tracy said, closing her eyes and smiling into the sun. "A woman could get used to this."

Mariah smiled, too. Although most of their communication had been by mail, she knew her friend all too well. Tracy would soon grow bored lazing around a swimming pool; before a week was past, she wouldn't be able to stand the inactivity. She'd be eager to get back to her job.

"You surprise me," Tracy said out of the blue.

"I do?" Mariah asked. "How?"

Tracy grinned sheepishly. "Well, when your parents first contacted me, they described you as this fragile rosebud who didn't have a clue about what she was letting herself in for."

"That's how they see me." It saddened Mariah to admit that. Her family's attitude was the very reason she'd left Seattle. They considered her helpless and inept, and if she'd stayed much longer she might have come to believe it herself.

"You really love it in Hard Luck, don't you?"

"Oh, yes. This has been the most..." Mariah hesitated, unsure how to explain what her year in the Arctic community had been like. She felt proud of her own ability to survive in difficult surroundings, especially during the winter when the temperature dropped to forty below zero. True, there were times she'd been lonely and confused. Depressed. At other times she'd felt a new confidence, a newly developed sense of self that was unlike anything she'd ever experienced. After a year in the Arctic, she knew she was capable of handling any situation. She'd learned to trust her own judgment and to take pride in her achievements.

But her nonrelationship with Christian continued to baffle her, although her attraction to him grew more potent with each passing month. Unfortunately he didn't seem to share her feelings. But then again, perhaps he did... The kiss gave her hope.

"When you told me you'd decided to stay in Hard Luck, I admired you," Tracy said with a thoughtful look. "I admired you for taking charge of your life and for not being afraid to do something risky."

Mariah squirmed under her praise. "It's no more than the other women have done—Abbey and Karen and Lanni. Bethany Ross and Sally Henderson."

"You're good friends with them, aren't you?"

"It's like they're part of my family," Mariah explained. But better. The women who'd come to Hard Luck were a close-knit group, out of necessity but also genuine liking. They relied upon and supported each other in every possible way. In the dead of winter, when sunlight disappeared and spirits fell, it was the women who brought joy and laughter to the community. She'd known these women for only a year, but her friendships with them were closer now than the friendships she'd left behind.

"What do you miss most?" Tracy asked next.

That question took some consideration. She wouldn't lie; there were certainly aspects of city life that she yearned for, services and stores and all kinds of things that weren't available in Hard Luck.

A number of items came to mind—first-run movies, her favorite junk food, shopping malls... "What do I miss most?" Mariah repeated slowly. "I'm thinking, Trace..."

"That, my friend, is answer enough," the attorney said. She sounded almost wistful.

CHRISTIAN SET ASIDE the murder mystery he was reading and forcefully expelled his breath. He couldn't seem to concentrate, although the author was one of his favorites.

Tomorrow evening, Mariah would be back, and frankly he dreaded her return. Despite his warning, he was sure she'd be foolish enough to put some stock in that stupid kiss. He tried to put her out of his mind, something he'd been struggling to do all week.

Mariah wasn't the only woman who'd been on his mind lately. Funny that he'd be thinking of Allison Reynolds now. But again and again he found himself comparing his current secretary with the one who got away.

Every time the statuesque blonde drifted into his thoughts, Christian felt his heart start to work like a blacksmith's bellows.

In the year since she'd returned to Seattle, he'd never called her. More fool he. When they first met, they'd dated—nothing serious, just a couple of dinners while he'd been in Seattle conducting business and setting up job interviews. He remembered those evenings with Allison in a haze of pleasure.

He was due to return to the Northwest, strictly for business purposes, anytime now. He'd been discussing the trip with Sawyer just that morning. Generally they took turns going to Seattle to arrange for supplies, but with Abbey pregnant and the kids getting ready to head back to school, Sawyer wasn't eager to leave Hard Luck. Christian was.

For one thing, he'd have a chance to visit his mother, who lived in Vancouver, British Columbia. He shared a special bond with Ellen. While Charles and Sawyer were more like their father in looks and temperament, Christian had always been closer to his mother.

As a boy, he'd spent eighteen months with her in England. The years before the separation had been a difficult time for his parents. Christian, only ten at the time, hadn't understood what was happening to his family.

All he knew, all he understood, was that his mother was desperately unhappy. More than once he'd found her weeping, and in his own way had attempted to comfort her. When she told him she was leaving Alaska, Christian had known immediately that he should go with her. His mother would need him, he thought—and she had.

Saying goodbye to his father and brothers was hard, and he'd missed them far more than he'd dreamed possible. In the beginning, he'd enjoyed living in England, but that hadn't lasted long. He missed Alaska. He missed his home, his brothers and the life he'd always known, and he suspected his mother did, as well.

After a year and a half, they'd flown back to Hard Luck, and for a time, a very brief time, they'd been a family again, and happy.

Christian had never fully understood what had shattered that fragile joy, but he realized Catherine Fletcher was somehow responsible. She was gone now and his father was, too. A few years ago Ellen had remarried; her second husband was a wonderful man who shared her passion for literature. She'd moved to his home in British Columbia.

Twice in the past year, Ellen had come to Hard Luck. Nevertheless, Christian intended to visit her and her husband, Robert, in Vancouver. He knew she was delighted with her new grandchildren, and if he could coordinate the flights, he might be able to bring Scott and Susan with him. A nice way to end their summer vacation. And Abbey and Sawyer could have a second honeymoon.

While he was in Seattle, Christian decided, he'd look up Allison Reynolds. The thought cheered him considerably. Yes, that was what he'd do. He'd give Allison a jingle and they'd go out on the town.

Content, Christian picked up the novel and started reading again. Then it struck him. It seemed unfair—and a bit unrealistic—to arrive in Seattle unannounced and expect Allison to be free.

Maybe he should call her now. Besides, talking to a woman who was as close to perfect as any human had a right to be was sure to lift his spirits.

In another moment, he'd dug out her phone number. The phone rang three long times. "Hello."

It was Allison. She sounded…silky. Yes, that was the right word for her voice—silky. Soft and a little breathless. A man could get light-headed just listening to her.

"Allison, this is Christian O'Halloran."

"Christian!" Her elevated voice said she was pleased to hear from him. "Don't tell me you're in Seattle? Why, I was just thinking about you the other day."

Forget light-headed, he was almost ecstatic. "You were?" Life was good. Very good.

"Are you in town?" The voice was definitely silky.

"No, but I will be."

"When?"

He couldn't believe how eager she sounded. "I'm not sure yet. I, uh, thought I'd arrange my schedule around yours. Are you going to be available this month?"

"I'm available any time you want." Her voice dipped in a playful whisper. Christian's chest tightened. This was one way to get Mariah out of his mind.

EARLY SATURDAY EVENING, Christian flew into Fairbanks to meet Mariah. He'd dreaded this moment all week, but now that it was upon him, he discovered that his earlier anxiety had vanished. He credited Allison with this. Knowing that a week from now he'd be spending time with the most beautiful woman he'd ever seen left him with a euphoric sense of well-being.

As he waited at the gate for Mariah's flight, he realized, somewhat to his surprise, that he was looking forward to seeing her again.

Sawyer was right; the office had been hectic without her to run interference, take calls, organize schedules and perform the dozens of other tasks she'd taken on. He'd admit it willingly. He suspected that he'd grown accustomed to having her around—and truth be known, he'd actually found himself missing her a time or two.

The gate where she was due to land was directly across from a gift shop. Deciding that this might be a good time to mend fences, Christian wandered inside. The instant he saw the small jade figurine he knew it was the perfect welcome-back gift. No larger than a child's building block, the green jade had been skillfully sculpted into a smooth bear, gripping a salmon between its teeth.

On impulse Christian bought it, then stuffed it in his pocket.

The flight landed on schedule, and Christian watched the passengers file out one by one. Mariah stepped out

of the jetway and glanced around expectantly, her arms
filled with packages. She looked tanned and rested.
When her gaze happened on him, she hesitated, as if
unsure of her reception.

Christian moved forward. "Welcome home," he said,
grinning.

"Hi. I wasn't sure you'd be here."

He chose to ignore the statement. "How was your
week?"

"Fantastic. Tracy and I had a fabulous time." She
shifted the packages in her arms. "I brought everyone a
small gift," she said, and lines of happiness crinkled at
the edges of her eyes. "Even you."

"That's funny, because I got you a gift, too. Just to
say glad you're back." He took some of the packages out
of her arms and together they headed toward the bag-
gage carousel.

"You bought me something?" She sounded incredulous.

Perhaps he should give it to her now, seeing that he'd
gone out of his way to make her life miserable for the
past twelve months. He found himself regretting his
earlier behavior toward her. Mariah wasn't so bad—once
he'd gotten used to working with her. Too bad that had
taken a year. "Have you had dinner?"

"Dinner," she repeated as if it were a foreign word.
She frowned and looked at him. "No. Are you sure
you're feeling all right?"

Christian chuckled. "I'm feeling just fine."

Once they'd retrieved her suitcase, he loaded that,
along with her carry-on packages, into the truck Midnight Sons kept at the airport.

He was turning over a new leaf as far as his relationship with Mariah was concerned. True, she was still an

irritant, but he was tired of fighting a losing battle. Sawyer thought she was wonderful, and so did almost everyone else. This week apart from her—and the prospect of seeing Allison—had done wonders for his tolerance.

"You're taking me to dinner?" she asked when he pulled into his favorite restaurant, the Sourdough Café. The ambience wasn't great, but the food more than made up for it.

"Sure," he said, and climbed out of the cab.

He led the way inside and selected a booth. Mariah sat across from him. Once he'd set his prejudices aside, he realized that she was a pleasant dinner companion. He laughed wholeheartedly at the tales of her escapades in Anchorage and carefully studied her photographs; she'd had them developed the day before. The most spectacular photos were of the boat tour she'd taken in Prince William Sound. Sometimes Christian forgot how impressive the glaciers were.

Mariah had captured the deep blue color of the ice with the sun glinting off the canyon's high walls. The marine-life photos—a pod of whales, several species of seals and a wide variety of birds—were as good as any he'd seen.

"These are wonderful pictures," he said enthusiastically.

She blushed with pleasure. "I'm sort of an amateur photographer."

He'd worked with her for more than a year now and hadn't known that.

Their meal arrived, and the conversation slowed momentarily while they dug into thick roast-beef sandwiches served on sourdough rolls.

It wasn't until they were back at the airport that Christian remembered the jade bear in his pocket.

He parked the truck and turned off the ignition.

"Thank you for dinner," she said, sounding almost shy.

"I'd like it if you and I could start over, Mariah," he said. He didn't want her to place any special significance on his words, but simply to take his offer at face value.

"I'd like that, too."

"I don't know what started us off on the wrong foot."

"Me, neither," she agreed.

"This last week—with you gone..." He hesitated, not knowing how to continue, not wanting to say too much.

"Yes?" she asked, her voice hushed.

"It didn't seem ... right."

If she was going to gloat, the time was now. To her credit she said nothing. "I've missed Hard Luck and all my friends. I ... missed you."

He wouldn't go so far as to admit he'd missed *her,* but she'd been on his mind. Removing the plastic sack from his flight jacket, he handed it to her. "I saw this at the gift shop in the airport and thought of you."

She carefully peeled away the tissue paper and gasped softly when she uncovered the tiny statue.

"Christian," she breathed in awe. "It's lovely. Thank you so much. I got you a silk scarf—nothing much. I read that early pilots needed them because oil used to spray into the open cockpit. The pilots cleaned their goggles with the scarves." She stopped abruptly, as if she realized she was chattering, and centered her attention on the jade bear.

"I wanted to apologize for being something of a jerk the past few months," he said. "This last week, with you away, I've come to see what a difference you've made at the office. You've come a long way since you first came to Hard Luck, Mariah.''

She looked up at him and to his astonishment, her eyes were bright with tears.

Tears.

''I'll be the first to admit that we've had our moments, but you've turned out to be an excellent secretary. You've become an important part of Midnight Sons.''

The tears spilled over, rolling down the sides of her face.

Christian wanted to tell her that the last thing he'd expected was emotion. He would have, too, if his mind hadn't been dominated by a more compelling thought. All at once, against every dictate of his will, he experienced the burning need to kiss Mariah Douglas again.

CHAPTER THREE

CHRISTIAN WAS ABOUT to kiss her. Mariah read the longing in his deep blue eyes and felt a rush of anticipation. Her hand closed around the precious jade figurine as she realized that her patience with Christian had finally paid dividends. She was about to receive her reward.

Her eyes drifted close as she awaited his touch. She'd dreamed of this moment, of exchanging gentle tender kisses and intense passionate ones. Now the dream was about to become reality.

Mariah waited for what seemed far too long. Nothing happened. Flustered, she opened her eyes and looked at him. To her amazement and utter embarrassment, she saw Christian sitting with his hands locked around the truck's steering wheel. His jaw was clamped tightly shut.

Mortified, Mariah swallowed and gathered her composure. Christian refused to kiss her? Well, so be it. She would resign herself to his cowardice. And her disappointment.

Still, Mariah had to acknowledge that he'd come a fair distance in the week she'd been away. He'd apologized for his childish behavior toward her and bought her the gift. For now that was enough. It would have to be.

The flight into Hard Luck seemed to take hardly any time. At first, the nonkissing incident left them feeling awkward and ill at ease, but after a year of sharing the office, they were familiar enough with each other that they quickly became comfortable companions once again.

By the time they approached the Arctic community, they were chatting amicably, like people with a number of shared friends and interests.

After Christian had parked and secured the aircraft, he loaded her suitcase and other packages into the company truck. "It's good to be home," Mariah whispered with a heartfelt sigh of appreciation. Her week away had been fun and relaxing, but she was grateful to get back to her normal life.

Although she insisted it wasn't necessary, Christian drove her to her small log cabin on the outskirts of town. He kept the engine running as he leapt out of the cab and carried her suitcase in. She noticed that he stopped abruptly just inside the door.

"Is something wrong?" she asked nervously, stepping up behind him.

"I'm surprised, that's all," he answered after a thoughtful pause.

"Surprised?"

"You've done a wonderful job with this place." Before she could ask what he meant, he elaborated. "Decorating the old cabin. Why, it's comfortable and downright homey."

"This *is* my home, Christian." She'd worked hard to make her space both livable and pleasing to the eye. That meant more than adding lace curtains to the windows. One of the first things she'd done was get rid of the chunky, oddly shaped furniture that came with the cabin. She'd replaced it, a piece at a time, with furniture that suited her needs—not the easiest task when you lived in the Arctic. She'd bought some chairs from Matt, had her bed shipped up from home, ordered fabric and a small table and a replica nineteenth-century oil lamp from catalogs. She had an eye for color and detail and was genuinely pleased with what she'd managed to achieve in her cramped quarters.

Christian set the suitcase down in the center of the room, on the green-and-rose braided rug she'd purchased on a trip to Fairbanks six months ago. She'd also splurged on a quilt that picked up the same colors.

"Thank you again," she said, rubbing her palms together. "I had a perfectly lovely evening. I appreciate your flying in for me, the dinner and...everything else."

He shrugged, looking uncomfortable with her gratitude. "I'll see you first thing Monday morning," he said a bit gruffly.

"Monday," she echoed.

As Christian walked past her, he paused and casually kissed her on the lips. He'd gone another couple of steps before he appeared to realize what he'd done. He came to a sudden halt, shook his head as if to clear it, then continued on to the truck.

MONDAY MORNING Mariah walked into the office and was greeted with chaos. Two phone lines rang simultaneously and the fax had started transmitting data. Christian was frantically searching through the filing cabinet, demanding to know where she'd hidden the Freemont account.

Concealing a smile, she located the file, answered the phone and dealt with the fax. It did her heart good to know she'd been missed.

"Welcome back," Sawyer told her two hours later. It was the first quiet moment that morning.

"Was it this hectic all week?" Mariah had barely had a chance to take off her sweater. The phone hadn't stopped ringing. Pilots had been coming and going every few minutes, and it seemed that they all needed something—a scheduling change, a form, some information. It hadn't helped matters that Christian was having a crisis of his own over the Freemont account. He spent much of the morning ranting and raving, unable to locate various crucial documents. Every time, it was Mariah who quietly and efficiently silenced him by supplying whatever he needed.

"We pretty much handled everything ourselves," Sawyer answered, "but we're sure glad you're back."

"You can say that again," Christian seconded, holding his hand over the mouthpiece. Sawyer glanced at his brother and then at Mariah. His eyes considered them shrewdly.

Mariah sat down and turned on her computer. The hard drive had started its familiar hum when Christian ended his telephone conversation and approached her desk.

"I'm going to need you to make travel arrangements for me," he told her.

"Of course." Christian would be traveling? Somewhat surprised, she reached for a pad and pencil.

"I'll be visiting my mother in British Columbia and then stopping off in Seattle."

"That won't be any problem. How long will you be away?" Reaching for the small calendar on her desk, she waited for him to give her the dates.

"Say, ten days from Friday—" he pointed to the end of that week "—until Sunday of the following week. And I'd like reservations at our usual hotel in Seattle. Oh, and Scott and Susan will be traveling with me as far as Vancouver. I'll go on to Seattle Monday or Tuesday, then back to Vancouver and home."

"I'll see to everything this afternoon," Mariah promised.

"While you're at it, could you give me the names of a couple of five-star Seattle restaurants?" Christian asked.

"Restaurants." She made a notation on her pad. "I know of a number in the downtown area that cater to businessmen." And Tracy would be happy to give her several suggestions, too.

"I wasn't thinking of a business dinner," Christian said matter-of-factly. "I'm going to be seeing a...friend while I'm in town. A good friend."

A few minutes later, Mariah was on the phone with the airline when she happened to overhear the two bothers talking.

"A friend?" Sawyer asked.

"Yeah, Allison Reynolds." Even from across the room, she saw Christian's eyes brighten with what could only be described as excitement. "You might remember her," he added.

Mariah felt as if she'd been slapped. No one needed to tell her who Allison Reynolds was—the secretary Mariah had replaced.

"You're going to be seeing Allison?" Sawyer asked, lowering his voice, obviously afraid Mariah would hear. Well, it was too late; she'd already heard.

"Yeah," Christian murmured, preoccupied with a fax. "I talked to her the other night and promised to get back to her as soon as I knew when I'd be arriving. With any luck, I'll convince her to give Hard Luck a second chance."

Sawyer held on to his pencil with both hands and darted a look toward Mariah. "Do you think that's wise?"

"Why isn't it?" Christian asked, his voice equally low. He set aside the fax and confronted his brother openly. "She's beautiful, witty, charming and we'd be fortunate to have her. Let's talk about this later, all right?"

Sawyer frowned.

Mariah couldn't believe her ears. Christian actually planned on luring her replacement to Hard Luck. Furthermore, he expected *her* to make the arrangements!

"MOM, SHOULD I PACK my Barbie playhouse?" Susan cried from her bedroom.

Abbey took the towel from the dryer, folded it and set it atop the washer. "No, sweetheart. You can only take one suitcase each. You won't have room for all your Barbie things."

"You know my mother's going to spoil those kids something terrible," Sawyer said, leaning against the laundry-room door.

"I know. Scott and Susan will be impossible to live with by the time they return."

"But we'll have an entire week to ourselves." Sawyer waggled his eyebrows suggestively. "I sincerely hope you intend to spoil *me* next week."

Abbey kissed her husband and nuzzled her nose against his. "I'll see what I can do."

Sawyer's eyes gleamed. "Barbie and Ken will play while the kids are away."

"Sawyer!"

Her husband chuckled and slid his arms around her waist. "It's too bad Christian will be gone, because that means I won't be able to get away much myself."

"We'll manage," Abbey assured him.

"A second honeymoon," Sawyer murmured, grinning provocatively. "I don't know if I'm up to this. I still haven't recovered from the first one."

"You seem to have done pretty well for yourself!"

"Mom, Dad, you'll remember to feed Eagle Catcher, won't you?" Scott asked, sticking his head into the laundry room.

Her son seemed genuinely concerned, as if he wasn't sure he should trust them with his much-loved friend, even if it was for only ten days. And even if he'd once been Sawyer's dog.

"We'll remember," she promised.

"It's important, Mom," Scott insisted. "This is only the second time we've been separated, and Eagle Catcher might worry. I had a long talk with him, but I'm not sure he understood."

"I promise we'll remember," Sawyer told him solemnly.

"Good." Scott looked relieved and disappeared.

Sawyer gently patted Abbey's protruding stomach. "This time alone will be good for us," he told her, his eyes serious. "After the baby arrives, everything will change."

Abbey knew her husband was right, but it would be a wonderful kind of change. So far the pregnancy had caused her almost no trouble, physically or emotionally. No morning sickness, no drastic mood swings. She loved Scott and Susan with the ferocity only a mother could understand, but their pregnancies had drained her. How different it was with Sawyer's baby. The comfort of his love, the assurance that he would move heaven and earth on her behalf, eased her worries.

"Mom!" Susan screeched from the hallway. "Should I pack my Bible?"

Abbey sighed and pressed her forehead against Sawyer's shoulder. "I'd better go supervise those two." She called to the kids that she'd be there in a minute.

"I'll finish up here for you," Sawyer said, gathering the rest of the towels from the dryer.

"Sawyer."

When he turned around, she leaned forward and kissed him with a hunger they generally reserved for the bedroom, playfully prodding the tip of his tongue with hers.

A low rumble of arousal came from her husband as she started to leave. Sawyer caught her hand. "What was that all about?"

She offered him a saucy smile. "Just a sample of what's available later."

"How much later?"

Abbey smiled again and stroked the side of his face. "As soon as the kids are gone, you and I can pick up where that left off." She walked out of the laundry room, but not before she noticed Sawyer staring at his wristwatch, calculating the hours before they'd be alone.

ALLISON REYNOLDS was as beautiful as Christian remembered. Even more so. Heads turned when they walked into the five-star restaurant. He'd never realized how much a beautiful woman could improve a man's image and raise his self-esteem. He had no doubt that he was the envy of every man there. Any vague, nagging thoughts about superficial values or shallow choices were easy enough to suppress.

He hadn't been in the Seattle hotel five minutes before he made a point of phoning Allison. He'd made

another phone call, too, but this one was to Hard Luck.
He'd had to call Mariah regarding a variety of subjects,
all having to do with the flight service.

It might have been his imagination, but her greeting
had seemed decidedly cool. He wasn't sure what to make
of her chilly tone, but whatever the problem, Sawyer
could handle it. As for him, he was taking a well-
deserved break from the office. He was willing to admit
privately that his business dealings, however necessary,
were a pretext; his primary reason for stopping in Seattle had to do with the beauty on his arm.

"I have a reservation for seven o'clock," Christian
informed the maître d'.

Allison smiled up at him sweetly, and it was all he
could do to pull his gaze away. He'd been mildly surprised by her dress; short and slinky, it revealed every
curve of her luscious body. Not that he minded. He
hadn't been able to take his eyes off her. But the front
was deeply cut, and that appeared to bring her a lot of
unwanted attention—unwanted, at least, by him. But he
was the one buying her dinner, and he wasn't all that
pleased to be sharing her, even vicariously, with anyone
else.

"This way," the man said, tucking two menus under
his arm. The restaurant had been one of Mariah's rec-
ommendations, and she'd chosen well. He'd have to remember to tell her that when he returned. The dim
interior suited him perfectly. Lights from the waterfront shimmered on the glass-smooth surface of Elliott
Bay. A ferry sailed in the distance, its lights blazing in the
night.

"This place is great," Allison said once they were
seated.

"My secretary chose it." He had to keep from telling Allison about Mariah. The stories would have them both in stitches, but he didn't want to spend the evening thinking about Mariah. Although her lack of friendliness earlier today continued to nag at him ...

Allison pressed the menu to her front and leaned forward. "I'm so glad you found someone else to work for you. Personally I can't imagine anyone lasting more than a day or so in that desolation."

Desolation. The Arctic? Hard Luck? Why, it was one of the most beautiful places on earth. Give him home any day of the week over the smog and traffic of the big city. Even a city as pleasing to the eye as Seattle. The noise factor alone had kept him awake most of the night. Street sounds had reverberated from the cluttered avenues and echoed against the skyscrapers. And in his expensive hotel, he'd heard the elevator and laughter in the halls and the TV next door. No wonder he felt suddenly tired and let down.

Christian roused himself. "What would you like?" he asked, studying the menu. He made his choice quickly. Blackened salmon, one of his favorites.

Allison's huge blue eyes met his. "I'm watching the calories, you know."

She seemed to wait for him to tell her that she was perfect as she was and that dieting would be ridiculous. Christian didn't. He'd never understood what it was about women and their weight. They seemed to feel it was a topic men found fascinating. Well, he, for one, found the subject boring. Nor did he think someone like Allison should need to fish for compliments.

"I'll have a salad," she said sweetly. "No dressing. You can't imagine how many grams of fat there are in salad dressing. Someone told me just the other day that it would be less fattening to eat a hot fudge sundae than to put dressing over lettuce. Can you imagine?''

Christian smiled benignly.

The waiter came for their order, and Allison took five minutes to give hers. She explained precisely how she wanted her salad. He'd never met a woman who requested sliced cucumbers on the side. And that wasn't all—she had to have her radishes cut a certain way and only on one-half of the salad. It amazed him that the waiter could write it all down and keep a straight face.

While Allison was giving her detailed instructions, the memory of his dinner with Mariah at the Sourdough Café came to mind. There'd been no talk of salad ingredients with her. Nor did she drag him into ridiculous conversations about grams of fat and hot fudge sundaes.

Unfortunately the dinner conversation didn't improve. Allison discussed the color of her fingernail polish in great detail. When Christian introduced another topic, she found a way of immediately bringing it back to herself and telling him about a new thigh cream on the market.

It became something of a game, watching how she was able to manipulate the conversation to reflect her own interests—such as they were. Not once did she ask him about the people she'd met on her brief trip to Hard Luck.

''Oh, I've got a new job now,'' she announced casually when he mentioned her old one. ''Actually this is the second job I've had in the past year.''

Christian nodded in seeming interest, and she went on, ''When I met you I was working for Pierce. He was a friend of my old boyfriend, Cary. But after I got back from Hawaii and went to see you, Pierce said he needed someone he could depend on. He'd never been pleased with me taking vacation time." She pursed her lips slightly. "He didn't even pay me my vacation days."

"How long did you work for Pierce?"

"About a month."

"A month. You didn't have vacation time due you."

"That's what Pierce said. Only he sounded really mad. You know, some men aren't the least bit nice. I worked for him one full month and his benefits were lousy."

Christian found it difficult to follow Allison's conversation from that point forward. Several times she mentioned names he didn't know and didn't care to know. Instead, his thoughts drifted to the year before, when he'd first met Allison. It astonished him that he hadn't seen through her then. The woman wasn't interested in working; she was looking for "benefits," and it seemed to him she wasn't just talking about paid holidays. She wanted a free ride.

When at last they'd finished their meal and were walking out of the restaurant, Christian was once again aware of several envious stares. Only this time it didn't raise his self-esteem. Sure, he'd enjoyed his blackened salmon, and the Washington-made wine had been some of the best he'd tasted, but he'd rather have eaten at Ben's or the Sourdough Café. As for his dinner companion, he hated to admit it, but he was disenchanted.

Later, when he dropped Allison off in front of her apartment, she flexed her long nails over his thigh. "Would you like to come up for a nightcap?" she asked. Her beautiful eyes invited him for more.

"Not tonight."

He helped her out of the car and walked her to her front door.

''When will I see you again?'' Her voice rolled from her lips like silk.

Christian had made the mistake of letting her know his schedule. ''I'll call you,'' he said.

She gave him a hurt-little-girl look. Her eyes rounded with a practiced look of disappointment. ''You will phone me, won't you, Chris? I'd be so unhappy if you didn't.''

Christian couldn't get away fast enough. They'd be raising huskies in hell before he'd agree to spending a second evening with the likes of Allison Reynolds.

After returning to his hotel room, Christian sat on the edge of the bed. It was hard to believe he'd been so blinded by her earlier. Because he was restless and angry, he reached for the phone and dialed Sawyer's home number.

''Hello,'' Sawyer answered impatiently.

''It's me.''

''Christian? Is something wrong? You don't sound like yourself.''

''I'm fine,'' he said, then wondered if that was true. Rarely had he felt so disappointed, so disillusioned, but he couldn't entirely blame his dinner date. His own willful blindness had something to do with it. ''You remember Allison, don't you?''

''Of course I remember her. Listen, little brother, if you're calling me to sing her praises, you've caught me at an inopportune moment. You seem to have forgotten Abbey and I are having our second honeymoon. She's decided to re-create the night we attended the luau. Grass skirt, leis, the whole deal. D'you mind if we talk about the sex goddess another time?''

''Trust me, Allison is no goddess.''

"Not you, honey," Christian heard his brother explain to Abbey. "I was talking about another sex goddess. One *far* less gorgeous than you."

"I'll talk to you when I get home," Christian promised. Chuckling to himself, he replaced the receiver.

A year ago, Christian had been completely wrapped up in Allison. He wasn't sure who'd changed in the past twelve months. Allison or him? But she wasn't the least bit how he remembered her.

A year ago, Christian had been thrilled when Allison had agreed, after some fast talking on his part, to give Hard Luck a try. Unfortunately, because of business commitments, he'd been unable to greet her personally when she'd arrived.

For an entire year he'd believed someone had said or done something to offend her. When he discovered she'd returned to Seattle after only one night in Hard Luck, he'd been furious. Not that there was anything he could do while he was on the road. He'd made one feeble attempt to contact her, but because he was busy with other things, he'd dropped the matter.

For twelve long months, he'd been convinced the people of Hard Luck had been at fault. The other women were jealous of Allison's natural beauty and had gone out of their way to make her feel unwanted. The list of possibilities had mounted—but there'd only been one reason Allison had left. A reason he hadn't seen until that very evening.

A vain, selfish woman wouldn't last more than a day in a town like Hard Luck. Allison had said it herself, although she'd meant something very different. And a day was exactly how long she'd stayed.

MARIAH THOUGHT she'd never been this miserable.
There wasn't enough deep-dish pizza in the world to get
her through the night, but that didn't keep her away
from the Hard Luck Café.

Christian was in Seattle dining with the beautiful, sophisticated Allison Reynolds. He didn't think she knew,
but she did, and that made everything worse.

Although she'd never met her, Mariah had heard everything she needed to know from the few women who
remembered Allison's brief visit.

Right that moment, Christian and Allison were at a
waterfront restaurant rated as one of the country's top
ten. Mariah didn't want to consider what the couple
would do following dinner. Dancing. Stargazing. Kissing. The thought of another woman in Christian's arms
was too painful to consider. Nor did she care to dwell on
how his relationship with Allison would affect her position with Midnight Sons.

She knew that Christian would do just about anything to get Allison back in Hard Luck.

Allison was a secretary. And so was she.

Given the choice, Christian would pick Allison over
her any day of the week. And she figured that, to keep
the peace, Sawyer would ultimately agree to letting her
go in favor of Allison.

"What can I do for you?" Ben asked.

Mariah sat at the table closest to the counter. "Do you
have any pizza left?"

"The ones with four kinds of cheese and all the ex-
tras?" He didn't wait for her to answer. "I suspect I've
got a couple tucked away in the freezer," he told her. "I
don't generally bake them up unless I have a special request."

"Would you be willing to consider this a special request?" Mariah asked. "This is a food emergency."

"A food emergency," Ben repeated, grinning. "Hey, I like that." He raised his hand and read the imaginary words, pointing one finger as he spoke. "Hard Luck Café, specializing in food emergencies." Then the amusement left his eyes, and he muttered, "It might go over better than my frequent-eater program."

"Could you feed me the pizza intravenously?" she joked, but it was a struggle.

Ben pulled out a chair and plopped himself down next to her. "What's the problem, kiddo?"

Mariah knew that a lot of the men in town talked to Ben; he was a good sounding board and a faithful friend. She liked and trusted him, but she wasn't comfortable talking about the situation between her and Christian. It didn't seem fair to unburden her soul to a friend of the O'Hallorans.

"I don't have anything one of your pizzas won't cure," she assured him.

"Coming right up." Ben stood and patted her affectionately on the shoulder. "You want anything to go with that?"

"Diet soda," she told him, knowing he'd find humor in her downing his million-calorie pizza with a diet drink.

"This could take a while," he said on his way to the kitchen. "The oven's got to heat up first."

"No problem."

Dirty lunch dishes sat on a couple of the tables, and because she felt too restless to sit there doing nothing, Mariah cleared off the tables.

"Thanks," Ben told her as she carried the dishes into the kitchen. "I meant to do that earlier."

"Anything else you need help with?" she asked.

"Nah."

But when she'd brought in the dishes from the second table, she noticed that some of the paper-napkin dispensers were empty. She asked Ben about that.

"I've been meaning to fill those, too, but I got sidetracked with everything else."

"I'll do it," she said, eager to occupy her hands while she waited for her food.

"I've been feeling a bit tired lately," Ben admitted. "Guess I'd better stop watching those late-night talk shows."

"I don't suppose you'd be needing extra help?" she asked hopefully. "Someone to wait tables, wash dishes, fill the napkin dispensers, that sort of thing."

"You serious?"

More than he knew. If everything went according to Christian's plan, her boss was about to lure the beautiful Allison Reynolds back to Hard Luck and offer her Mariah's job.

"I'm very serious," she told Ben.

"Actually I've been thinking about getting some help for a while now. In fact, I was about to ask Christian to pass along a handful of the applications he collected last year."

"I thought business was, uh, down a bit." She spoke as tactfully as she could. She'd heard that a decrease of customers was the reason he'd started the frequent-eater program.

"It's not so bad lately," Ben said, leaning against the counter. "I'm here 365 days of the year. You can't blame a man for wanting a break now and again. Have you got someone in mind for the job?"

Mariah nodded.

"Who?"

She didn't hesitate. "Me."

"You?"

Despite her best efforts, her lower lip quivered slightly. "Christian's in Seattle and he . . . he's with Allison Reynolds."

"Listen, Mariah, I don't know what he sees in that woman, but trust me, your position with Midnight Sons is safe! Sawyer isn't going to let him replace you with anyone."

"I've known for a long time that Christian would like to be rid of me."

"I'm not saying whether that's true or not, but I *will* say that his attitude underwent a . . . minor adjustment in the week you were away."

"Well, that's nice," she murmured a little sarcastically. "But he'd do *anything* to convince Allison to move here. He's been stuck on her all year."

Ben didn't argue. As he often did, he rubbed the side of his jaw. "I don't know what to advise you."

"If you don't hire me, maybe Pete Livengood will," she rushed to say. "It seems to me that he might need someone to stock shelves for him."

"Now don't do anything rash," Ben said, and patted her hand. "Sawyer's always been on your side, no matter how much Christian griped."

Which was another way of telling her that Christian had done plenty of griping.

The oven buzzed in the background. "Let me get your pizza into the oven and I'll be right back," Ben told her, scurrying to the kitchen.

She could always apply for a position with the state, too, she mused while he was gone. But if she got a job, it was unlikely she'd be able to continue living in Hard Luck, which made the idea less appealing.

"You're sure you'd want to work in a restaurant?" Ben asked when he returned. His look was thoughtful.

"I'm positive." The way she saw things, she soon wouldn't have a choice.

"If you feel you don't want to stay with Midnight Sons anymore, you can have a job right here."

CHAPTER FOUR

THE LUMP in Mariah's throat felt like the size of a grapefruit. The computer screen blurred as her eyes filled with unshed tears. Swallowing hard, she quickly typed out her letter of resignation. Every word was like the end of a dream, the end of her hopes. The printer spewed out the single sheet, and she took a few minutes to compose herself before signing it.

When Mariah was fairly certain she wouldn't make a fool of herself by bursting into tears, she brought the letter to Sawyer.

"What's this?" he asked, glancing up from his computer terminal.

"I'm giving you my notice."

Sawyer's gaze shot to hers in disbelief. "You're quitting?"

She nodded, then said with forced cheerfulness. "It's been a wonderful experience, but as Christian pointed out, my contract is up. I'd agreed to work for Midnight Sons for a year, and—" she shrugged "—it's time to move on."

"Is it the money?" Sawyer asked with a dumbfounded look. "Are you unhappy with the benefits package?"

"No. You've always been more than generous."

"But..." Sawyer didn't seem to know what to say. She realized she'd taken him by surprise, but that couldn't be helped. She'd made her decision, felt it was the right one.

"In that case, can I ask why you want to leave?" Sawyer asked. "Especially now?"

"For one thing, I can see the writing on the wall," she told him, struggling to keep her voice even. "I overheard Christian telling you he wants to bring Allison Reynolds back to Hard Luck. There simply isn't enough work to occupy two full-time secretaries. Allison was the one he wanted from the first. I . . . I have what I want—the cabin and the twenty acres of land."

"Now, listen, there's no way in hell I'm going to let my brother hire Allison Reynolds," Sawyer insisted. "Your position here is secure, I promise you." Fire glowed in his eyes as if battle loomed on the horizon and he was ready to take aim. Brother against brother.

"I appreciate what you're saying, and I thank you, but you and I both know that Christian—"

"It's not going to happen, Mariah," Sawyer said between clenched teeth. "I won't let it."

He was making this far more difficult than she'd anticipated. She'd assumed she'd hand in her notice, and he'd put up a token fuss, then release her. What surprised her was the vehemence with which he argued.

"Thank you, Sawyer. I'm grateful for what you're trying to do, but the last thing I want is to cause dissension between you and Christian. We both know he'd prefer to work with Allison."

"Why don't we wait until Christian's back?" he suggested. "There's no need to jump to conclusions. I talked to him just last night, and he didn't mention bringing Allison back with him." He paused and seemed to reconsider. "But then, I suppose I didn't give him much of an opportunity to say much."

"It's too late, Sawyer. I already have another job."

This seemed to shock him even more. His jaw dropped and his eyes widened. "Who...where...when?"

"The Hard Luck Café. I'm going to work for Ben."

"Since when did Ben Hamilton need a secretary?" Sawyer demanded. He made it sound as if Ben had stolen her away from him.

"Not a secretary," Mariah hurried to explain. "He needs help in the kitchen."

"You're qualified to cook?"

"I won't be responsible for the cooking," she clarified. "I'll wait tables and help in other areas, too. Ben's been running the café on his own all these years. It's time he relaxed and left the small stuff to someone else."

"Ben!" Sawyer said the name in a tone that implied his longtime friend had turned traitor.

"*I* asked *him* about the job," Mariah pointed out. She didn't want to cause trouble between Ben and the O'Hallorans any more than she wanted to between the two brothers.

Sawyer reread her letter and frowned anew. "You're sure this is what you want?"

Was she sure? Mariah didn't know anymore. From what Christian and the others had said, Allison Reynolds was a real beauty; he was obviously completely besotted with her. Mariah didn't stand a chance of winning Christian's heart. It wasn't easy to walk away from this job—or from Christian—but she had to, for the sake of her sanity. And for the sake of her pride, she had to convince Sawyer she was perfectly content to give up her duties with Midnight Sons. She had to be certain he'd never know how much it hurt.

"I'm sure," she said, revealing nothing.

Sawyer pinched the bridge of his nose. "In that case there's not much I can say."

"WHAT DO YOU MEAN, Mariah quit?" Christian shouted into the telephone.

"She handed me her notice first thing this morning," Sawyer said, sounding none too pleased with the turn of events.

"She can't do that!"

"Why can't she?" Sawyer asked impatiently. "It's a free country. We can't force her to work for Midnight Sons if she doesn't want to."

Christian stood, forgetting that the receiver was connected to the telephone on the hotel nightstand. He started to pace and the phone fell with a discordant clang. For an instant Christian feared he'd severed the connection.

"You there?" he demanded of his brother.

"Yes. What happened?"

"Nothing. I dropped the phone." Christian rammed his fingers into his dark blond hair and winced at the unexpected twinge of pain. "You might have tried talking some sense into her."

"I talked until I was blue in the face. I tried everything short of out-and-out bribery. I have to tell you, Christian, I blame *you* for this. You haven't done a damn thing to help, you know."

"How the hell can I help when you're in Hard Luck and I'm in Seattle?" His irritation was fast turning to anger. This whole business with Mariah didn't make sense. It should've been obvious to Sawyer—to anyone with half a brain—how crucial it was to keep Mariah with Midnight Sons. She knew more about the office than the two brothers combined. True, there'd been a time, not so long ago, when he'd have willingly replaced her. But he'd experienced a change of heart in the week she'd been away. And the week *he'd* been away...

"It seems to me I'm the one stuck here with all the problems," Sawyer said, his voice hard. His patience was clearly as short as Christian's. "As I recall, last year about this time you were off in Seattle dating your cover model, and I was left to deal with an avalanche of problems you'd created. It's the same thing all over again."

"Now just a minute—"

Sawyer didn't allow him to finish. "You'd better remember exactly whose idea it was to bring women to Hard Luck in the first place."

"Yeah, but if it wasn't for me you'd never have met Abbey." Christian played his trump card before this argument with his brother could deteriorate any further.

Sawyer sighed deeply, and Christian could virtually hear his anger drain away. "True."

"I'll talk to Mariah myself," Christian said, feeling confident he'd succeed where his brother had failed. If she'd listen to anyone, it would be him. He felt they'd come to an understanding in the last little while. Mended fences and all that.

"Fine, but you should know that it's because of you she's decided to quit."

"Me?" Sawyer must have misunderstood. His relationship with Mariah had taken a dramatic turn for the better. Or so he'd assumed. This bit of news didn't make sense.

"She seems to think you're bringing Allison back with you, so she's stepped aside."

"You're joking! What made her think that?"

Sawyer's frustration was palpable. "You did, little brother. You managed all this single-handedly."

"Me? How?"

"You told me you planned to talk Allison into giving Hard Luck another shot."

He'd said that? Christian pressed his hand against his brow. "Well, I didn't. She's not coming."

Christian's words were followed by a stiff silence. "That wasn't the impression you gave me," Sawyer eventually said. "And apparently Mariah overheard the conversation."

Christian cursed.

"Mariah felt that if Allison returned to Hard Luck, there wouldn't be enough work for two full-time secretaries."

"You'd better let me talk to Mariah," Christian muttered. "I'll straighten all this out in short order."

"It's too late," Sawyer said with a heavy sigh. "She's already got another job. Apparently she and Ben have come up with this scheme—"

"Mariah and *Ben?*"

"Right. She's going to be his assistant, help in the kitchen, wait tables, that sort of thing."

"You've got to be kidding!"

"I swear it's true."

"Let me talk to her," Christian demanded again. He could foresee trouble already—for Ben, as well as for Midnight Sons. Apparently Ben hadn't remembered how clumsy Mariah was. He'd never known a woman more inclined to trip over her own two feet.

"She isn't here," Sawyer murmured. "I have a feeling we're going to lose the best damn secretary we ever had, and frankly, Christian, I hold you responsible."

This didn't seem to be the moment to remind Sawyer that Mariah was the first and only secretary Midnight Sons had ever had.

No one responded to Bethany's knock at the back door of the Hard Luck Café. She tried again, then turned the knob—the door was open. She let herself inside.

"Ben?" she called.

No answer. A sliver of light peered out from beneath the doorway that opened to the stairs leading to Ben's private quarters.

Bethany opened the door and peered up the stairway. "Ben," she called again. Smiling to herself, she climbed the stairs. More than likely he was asleep in his chair.

She was right. He lay stretched out on the recliner, the television guide spread across his lap. His head was tipped back, mouth open, and he was snoring lightly.

"Ben." Bethany pressed her hand over his.

His eyelids fluttered open, and he blinked a couple of times. "Bethany? What time is it?"

"Nine."

"Nine," he repeated. "That's early yet."

"Yes, I know."

He leaned forward slightly, yawning, then reached for the television controller and pushed the Power button. "I must've fallen asleep. Guess I'm beginning to feel my age. Soon I'll be an old man."

Shaking her head, Bethany sat down on the love seat. "Not you. Never you."

It was easy to see that her words pleased him. "It's good to see you. Now, to what do I owe the pleasure?"

She slipped off her shoes and tucked her feet beneath her. "Mitch's on patrol and Chrissie's spending the night with a friend. She's been beside herself not knowing what to do with Susan O'Halloran on vacation. Those two have gotten so thick that Chrissie's lost without her. I think it's a good idea for her to make other friends."

"Are you ready for school?" Ben asked.

"Yes. No," Bethany quickly amended, and then because she couldn't hold the news inside any longer, she blurted it out. "I'm pregnant."

Ben's feet slid off the recliner and slapped the floor. "Pregnant!"

"Mitch and I are just as amazed—almost." She nearly laughed aloud at his incredulous look.

"But you've only been married a few weeks."

"I know. We didn't plan to have a baby this soon, that's for sure. It was just... one of those things."

Ben's eyes lit up. "Unplanned pregnancies are sometimes the very best kind," he said, nodding sagely.

Bethany knew he was referring to her own birth. He'd had an affair with her mother before leaving for Vietnam, and because of a disagreement, he'd never known Marilyn was pregnant. He'd never known of his daughter's existence. Bethany had learned Peter Ross wasn't her biological father while she was in college, after her mother had experienced a cancer scare. As the years progressed, Bethany had become increasingly curious about the man who'd fathered her. With a bit of detective work and the help of the American Red Cross, she'd been able to trace Ben to Hard Luck.

Soon afterward, she'd applied for a teaching position in the tiny Arctic community, hoping to meet him.

Bethany had never planned to confront Ben with the truth, but she was relieved—and happy—that she had. In many ways they were very alike, and in others dissimilar. No one in town, other than her husband, knew Bethany's true relationship to Ben, although she wondered how it was no one had guessed. Ben was fiercely proud of her and staunchly protective; she felt the same about him.

"A baby," Ben repeated, grinning broadly. "How does Mitch feel about this?"

"When I first told him, he was floored, but it didn't take him long to adjust to the idea. The baby's due in May, about the same time school gets out, so the timing's good. We told Chrissie about the baby this evening, and she went nuts. I can tell she's going to be a wonderful big sister."

"Have you told your mother and father?"

"Oh, yes, first thing. They're thrilled."

"I'm thrilled for you, too, sweetheart."

"It still takes some getting used to. I'm just becoming accustomed to being a wife and stepmom, and now I'm about to be a mother."

Ben chuckled. "Try finding out that you're a father at my age—that's what I call a bombshell. As for this little one, well, I'd tend to think of your baby as a delightful surprise."

"Now," Bethany said, relaxing against the back cushions, "what's this wild rumor I've been hearing about your taking on an assistant?"

"It's true," Ben said, more satisfied with hiring Mariah every time he thought about it. "Mariah Douglas is coming to work with me."

"But...I thought she was the secretary for the O'Hallorans."

"She is—was. What I understand, she's already handed in her notice. Sawyer's annoyed with me, but it's not my fault—Mariah approached *me*. The way I figure it, she already had her heart set on leaving Midnight Sons. I tried to convince her to stay with the O'Hallorans, but she wouldn't hear of it."

"You'd think Christian would be pleased. He's been looking for a way to be rid of her from the moment I met him," Bethany recalled.

"Apparently he's had a change of heart."

"Isn't that just a like a man?" Bethany muttered, shaking her head. "They don't know *what* they want."

CHRISTIAN THOUGHT he'd never been this eager to get back to Hard Luck. In the past several days he'd talked to Sawyer half-a-dozen times. Every time, he'd hung up frustrated—and confused.

As far as he could grasp, Sawyer had released Mariah from serving out her full two-week notice, and the woman his brother had referred to as "the best secretary they'd ever had" was gone.

Scott and Susan were just as eager to be home. Christian had collected them from his mother's, and Ralph Ferris flew into Fairbanks to meet their commercial flight. The short hop between Fairbanks and Hard Luck felt longer than the flight from Vancouver to Anchorage.

By the time the plane touched down in Hard Luck, Christian had his conversation with Mariah all figured out.

Sawyer and Abbey were at the airfield waiting for Scott and Susan. The kids leapt out of the plane and raced toward their parents, both chattering a mile a minute, eager to share their experiences with Grandma Ellen and Grandpa Robert.

Christian waited impatiently for a moment alone with Sawyer. "Where is she?" he asked abruptly.

Sawyer blinked at him, wearing a baffled expression. "Oh, you mean Mariah."

Who else would he have been referring to? "Yes, I mean Mariah."

"Ben's, I'd guess. She spends every day there, now that she no longer works for us." Judging by the edge in Sawyer's voice, he still seemed to place the blame squarely on Christian's shoulders. He'd settle the issue with his brother later, Christian decided.

"Who's minding the office?" Surely Sawyer wasn't so irresponsible as to leave it unattended. The flight service had grown by thirty percent in the past year, thanks partly to the boom in population. An answering machine no longer met their needs, and Sawyer knew that.

"Lanni's agreed to step in for now, but she's got her own work, you know. I told her it wouldn't take *you* long to find Mariah's replacement."

"Me?" he exploded. He leaves for a few measly days, and his brother lets all hell break loose, then calmly announces it's *his* responsibility to set everything right.

"Yeah, you," Sawyer returned, eyes snapping. "If you'll recall, you spent the better part of a month interviewing job applicants. I don't even know where you filed the résumés."

"I didn't file them. Mariah did."

"Ask her, then. All I can say is we need to hire someone and quick. It isn't fair to Lanni to keep her tied up at the office. She's got better things to do with her time than answer our phones."

"You might have discussed it with me first," he argued.

"I would've if you'd been here," Sawyer said in a disgusted voice.

Christian didn't deign to respond. It was clear that he wasn't going to get anywhere with Sawyer when his brother was in this cantankerous frame of mind. Sawyer unfairly blamed him for Mariah's sudden need to become a waitress. Well, he wasn't going to accept the blame for that.

As soon as Christian had dropped off his suitcase at home, he headed to the Hard Luck Café. First thing he noticed when he walked in the door were the table-cloths—not plastic, either. A vase of wildflowers on each table added a touch of color and warmth. On the chalk-board, where Ben wrote the daily dinner special, some-one had drawn yellow daisies.

Ralph Ferris sat at one of the tables, reading over the menu, which also looked new. They acknowledged each other with a brief nod.

Christian stepped up to the counter the way he al-ways did and pulled out a stool. He nearly slid onto the floor—the stools had been newly padded and recovered in shiny black vinyl.

It certainly hadn't taken Mariah long to leave her mark on the café.

She was busy making coffee, and apparently didn't hear him come in.

"Did you want coffee?" she called to Ralph over her shoulder.

"Please," Ralph called back.

Mariah turned with a full pot in her hand—and saw Christian sitting at the counter. She gave a start, and the glass carafe slipped from her fingers. It shattered, and hot coffee splashed across the polished floor.

"Oh, no!" Luckily Mariah had leapt back in time to avoid getting burned.

It took a determined effort on Christian's part not to jump to his feet and call attention to the accident. He merely shook his head. Poor Ben. He hadn't a clue what he was letting himself in for when he hired Mariah.

"What happened?" Ben stuck his head out from the kitchen.

"I—I broke the coffeepot."

Christian waited for the cook to start bellowing. Ben wasn't known for his patience, and if ever a woman was born to try men's souls, it was Mariah Douglas.

He'd give Ben a week; then he'd be begging Christian and Sawyer to take her off his hands.

"Don't worry about it," Ben said, reaching for the mop. "I've got plenty of pots. You weren't burned, were you?"

"No. I'm fine." Her eyes flew to Christian, narrowing as if she blamed *him* for the accident. He hadn't done a damn thing, yet everyone in Hard Luck was ready to go for his jugular.

"Your coffee'll be just a minute," Mariah told Ralph.

"No problem," the bush pilot assured her. He unfolded the Fairbanks newspaper and disappeared behind it.

"I'll take a cup when you get around to it," Christian said, righting the ceramic mug in front of him. He might be risking his life asking her to pour it for him, but it was a risk he'd have to take.

Mariah refilled another glass pot from the large coffee percolator. He noted that her hand shook slightly as she filled his mug. "When did you get back?" she asked conversationally. Christian wasn't fooled; she'd been the one to arrange his itinerary. She knew his travel schedule as well as he did.

"This afternoon."

Mariah pulled an order pad from her apron pocket. "What can I get you?"

"I'll have a piece of apple pie."

Mariah called back the order to Ben, who appeared a couple of minutes later with a large slice of pie. He set it in front of Christian and eyed him warily, as if anticipating a confrontation.

Christian thought smugly that he didn't need to say a word. Within a week, when Ben was out of coffeepots and patience, he'd recognize that Mariah was never cut out to be a waitress.

"How's it going?" Christian asked Ben, tipping his head toward Mariah, who was busy serving Ralph his lunch. It looked as if he'd ordered the day's special—meatloaf sandwich, with a bowl of beef-and-barley soup.

"With Mariah?" Ben grinned. "Great. Just great." He gestured toward the tables. "Have you ever seen my place look better? Mariah's responsible for all the fancy touches. I don't know why I delayed hiring someone for so long. She's the best thing that's happened to the café since I got in the soft-ice-cream machine."

Christian took a bite of the pie and raised his brows. "Hey, this is good. What's different?"

"Mariah baked it."

"Mariah?" Ben could've knocked him over with a flick of his finger.

"It's her grandmother's recipe. Best damn apple pie I've ever tasted. As far as I'm concerned, she can do all the baking around here, she's that good."

Christian was confused, to put it mildly. "Are you sure we're talking about the same Mariah?"

Ben chuckled. "I'm sure." The cook drifted back to the kitchen, but Christian wasn't alone for long. Mariah hurried to bring him the small canister of cream.

"I—I forgot you like your coffee with cream, don't you?"

Christian didn't bother to correct her. "Do you have a minute?" he asked.

She hesitated. "The dinner crowd will start coming in any time now."

It was barely four; a poor excuse. "I'd appreciate it if you could sit down and chat for a few minutes."

"All right." But her reluctance was obvious. She walked around the counter to sit on the stool next to him. Folding her hands on the counter, she waited for Christian to speak.

"Allison didn't come back with me," he said, wanting to clear the air about that immediately. He understood her concern and was willing to admit that he'd been sadly remiss in mentioning the other woman in Mariah's presence. He'd seen the error of his ways; now he wanted her back. They'd just begun to find their footing with each other, and it seemed a shame to end it all so abruptly. And unnecessarily.

Three months ago, hell, three weeks ago, he would've openly cheered to see her leave Midnight Sons. But not now.

"Sawyer already told me she wouldn't be coming." Her gaze met his straight on.

"Then why'd you decide to quit?"

"It never really worked out between you and me."

"Things were improving, though, don't you think?"

"I suppose. Only you . . ." She hesitated.

"Yes?" he pressed.

"You wanted a different secretary."

"I don't anymore," he said, growing impatient. It occurred to him to tell her he'd made a mistake, to apologize, but he couldn't quite bring himself to do it.

"I'm already committed to working for Ben," she said, and she did sound mildly regretful. "Do you like the pie?"

At the moment it stuck in his throat, but he managed to respond with a quick nod.

"So your mind's made up?" he asked, pushing back his plate.

"Yes." She eyed him expectantly, and it occurred to him that she was waiting for him to plead with her. Well, there'd be frost in the Caribbean before he'd grovel! If she didn't want to work for Midnight Sons, fine. There were stacks of applications from women clamoring for the opportunity to move north. He'd met a number of them himself a year ago.

"Fine." He stood and paid for the pie. "We're sorry to see you go, but what the hey, right? You were with us a year and it was fun."

"Yes," she said, but she didn't sound so sure that it *was* fun.

Christian walked back to the mobile office. Their conversation hadn't gone nearly as well as he'd assumed it would. Perhaps he should've waited a day or two. Rushing over to Ben's the minute the plane landed made him look too eager; that had been a tactical error. Still, he had other options, and he planned to exercise them, starting now.

Christian opened the top drawer of the filing cabinet and sorted through a sequence of file folders, searching for the one that contained the applications he'd received the summer before. It took a while, but he soon located what he needed, and without any help from Mariah.

With the precious folder tightly clutched in his hand, he walked over to his desk and sat down. Reading through the top three instantly lifted his spirits. Plenty of women had been eager for this position.

"Ramona Cummings," he said aloud, remembering his interview with the dark-haired beauty immediately. Gleefully he punched out the phone number.

Disconnected.

Christian flipped to the second application. "Rosey Stone." A face didn't come to mind, but he'd probably remember her once he heard her voice. Once again he punched in the number and waited.

A soft, feminine voice answered.

"This is Christian O'Halloran from Hard Luck, Alaska. Is Rosey Stone available?"

"This is Rosey." She sounded surprised and a little breathless. Good, Christian liked awed and breathless. This was a fine start, a fine start indeed.

"You applied for the position of secretary last year."

"Yes . . . yes, I remember!" she said excitedly.

"We currently have a position available, and we'd like to offer it to you." He felt smug at the thought that it would be such a snap to replace Mariah.

"Are you still offering the same employment package you were a year ago?" Rosey asked.

"Ah...yes. There's a cabin available. Actually it isn't much," he added with a twinge of conscience. "My father built it over thirty years ago, and there's no electricity and no indoor plumbing."

"You're joking!"

Christian didn't know what had possessed him to blurt that out. "The cabin lacks all modern conveniences." He smacked his forehead with one hand, wondering if he had a temperature.

"What is this, some kind of sick joke?"

"No. The job's available if you still want it."

"No, thanks," she informed him primly, and slammed the phone down in his ear.

"I didn't think you would," he said into the drone of the disconnected line. Sighing, Christian hung up the receiver. Damn it all, he wanted Mariah back.

CHAPTER FIVE

BRIGHT AND EARLY Monday morning, Christian settled down at his desk in the Midnight Sons office. Determined to make some headway in replacing Mariah, he reached for the file folder containing the pertinent applications.

Leaning back comfortably in his chair, he read over a number of résumés. Several applicants were vastly overqualified. Others had little or no relevant experience, just a certain eagerness for adventure. Unsure if he should trust them, Christian decided they wouldn't work out, either. Neither Sawyer nor he had time to train a replacement.

Discouraged, he set the file aside and promised himself he'd read through it again later, when he was mentally ready to deal with the problem. What he wanted of course, what he hoped would happen, was that Mariah would realize she wasn't cut out for the restaurant business and return to Midnight Sons. Now that she knew Allison Reynolds wouldn't be coming, there was no reason to be stubborn.

Sawyer arrived a half hour after Christian and seemed surprised to find his brother at the office so early.

"I've been working on finding a replacement for Mariah," Christian told Sawyer. What he failed to mention was that he hadn't found a résumé or application that suited him yet. Nor did he think it was a good idea to admit he was holding out, hoping Mariah would have a change of heart.

"Good," Sawyer answered sharply.

"You want to give me some help here?" He supposed they might as well go through the motions. "Perhaps we should go for an older woman this time, someone mature," he suggested.

"Sure." Sawyer didn't sound as if he particularly cared.

"Someone who's methodical," Christian said next. "I don't care how fast she types, as long as she's accurate." He wrote that down on the pad.

"Sounds good to me," Sawyer murmured while assembling a pot of coffee.

The coffee had always been made before they arrived at the office—by Mariah. Not that they weren't capable of making coffee themselves. But it was thoughtful of her to do it without being asked. Christian hadn't given the matter more than a passing thought until just that moment. In fact, Mariah had taken on a number of small tasks that made their lives easier.

"She should have a good attitude," Christian went on.

"I agree," Sawyer said with conviction. "I don't want someone to come in here asking what we can do for her. I'm much more interested in what she can do for us, especially since we're the ones paying her wages."

Christian added "good attitude" to the list, and with Sawyer's help came up with several other qualities. They found it vital that the new secretary be prompt and professional. Loyal and responsible. Because they did so much of their business over the phone, a good phone manner was essential.

As Christian read over the qualifications for Mariah's replacement, it became obvious that—except for the "older" part—they'd described Mariah herself.

Christian felt suddenly troubled. How could he have been so...so misguided? The perfect candidate had been there all along, and it had taken him all this time to see it. For twelve months he'd been hoping she'd leave; now that she was gone, he wanted her back. Something was definitely wrong, and he had the feeling whatever was askew had to do with him.

"Have you found someone yet?" Sawyer asked no more than ten minutes later.

"No!" Christian snapped. "How could I?"

"Well, read through those applications, would you? The sooner we can get someone here, the better. We can't expect Lanni to fill in for long."

"I understand that," Christian returned impatiently.

"Charles was against Lanni coming to work for us in the first place," Sawyer went on, "but she insisted a few days from her writing wouldn't matter. She'll be in this afternoon."

Christian didn't understand why Sawyer was in such an all-fired hurry. He'd already gone through the file a second time and hadn't found a suitable applicant. Nor did he share his brother's sense of urgency. This wasn't something that needed to be done right that very minute.

Brother worked amicably with brother the remainder of the morning. Their staff of pilots wandered in and out of the office, as was their habit, before heading out to the hangar to complete their assignments for the day.

"Who's going to make up the flight schedule?" Sawyer asked.

In the past Mariah had seen to it.

"You do it this week and I'll do it next," Christian offered in what he felt was a fair compromise.

"You'll do it next week," Sawyer muttered sarcastically. "You'd better have hired a replacement long before then."

Before next week! Hell and damnation, Sawyer didn't actually expect someone to drop her entire life because of a phone call, did he? It wasn't likely Christian would find a replacement willing to move to the Arctic just like that. These things took time, lots of time.

Duke Porter was the last pilot to stop off at the office that morning. He walked in, glared at Christian and announced, "Mariah's working at Ben's."

"Yes, I know." Christian studied the pilot. Although Mariah had assured him there was nothing between Duke and her, Christian couldn't help wondering.

"Why?" Duke still glared at him.

"You'll have to ask her." Christian wouldn't mind having the answer to that himself.

"I'm asking you," Duke said in a way that laid the blame directly on Christian's shoulders.

"I don't know why she quit," he mumbled, and realized that wasn't entirely true. "I have my suspicions, but none I'd care to discuss."

"It isn't the same around here without Mariah," Duke complained, setting aside his clipboard. "A man becomes accustomed to things being done a certain way."

"What do you mean?" Sawyer asked. "It's still the same office, same business."

"Well, for one thing it's too quiet in here. A man could get, I don't know, bored coming here these days."

"Bored," Sawyer repeated.

"Bored," Duke said again, with more certainty this time. "Before, it was fun to watch Mariah tiptoe around

Christian. She used to make these hilarious faces at him behind his back."

"She did what?" Christian was outraged, then amused. That sounded like something she'd do, and in retrospect he didn't hold it against her. He *had* been something of a jerk.

"Who could blame her?" Duke asked. "For making faces *or* leaving. Christian was always on her case for one reason or another, but she was a good sport about it." He turned to Christian. "Everyone knew you were looking for an excuse to fire her. But without Mariah around, it's... it's like someone dimmed the lights in here."

Christian was inclined to argue, but realized Duke spoke the truth. In more ways than one.

"Do you?" Duke pressed. "Blame her for leaving?"

"I guess I can't," Christian admitted in a grudging voice.

The pilot seemed surprised that Christian had agreed so readily. "You going to get her back?"

Christian desperately hoped so, but he couldn't guarantee anything. With luck, Mariah would realize waitressing wasn't for her. She had all kinds of abilities that were wasted at the café although he had to concede she baked a fine apple pie.

Duke left after a few more admonitions, and Christian started thinking about what the bush pilot had said. He sure as hell wasn't going to plead with her to come back, but that didn't mean he wasn't willing to make a few subtle suggestions.

"Will you be all right if I drop in at Ben's for a few minutes?" he asked his brother.

Sawyer gave him an odd look, then nodded. "Just don't be too long."

"I won't."

He hurried across the yard and noticed a distinctive chill in the air. Although it was still August and summer wasn't officially over, he could feel autumn coming on; soon the days would shorten dramatically. It wasn't unheard of for snow to fall in September or for the rivers to freeze. The wind increased as he rushed into the Hard Luck Café, almost pulling the door out of his hand. He saw Ben at the counter; the place was otherwise empty, since coffee break was over and the lunch crowd hadn't started to arrive yet.

Ben offered Christian a friendly smile. "What can I do for you this fine day?" he asked.

"How about coffee and a doughnut?" Christian pulled out a stool. He made sure that when he sat down this time he didn't slide off. He looked around, wondering where Mariah was, but he didn't want to be so obvious as to ask.

"In the kitchen. Baking another pie," Ben supplied, knowing all too well the purpose of Christian's visit.

Christian pretended not to know what Ben was talking about.

"You want me to call her out here?" Ben offered.

"No," Christian answered automatically, then regretted it.

"She's causing quite a stir, you know," Ben said conversationally as he filled Christian's mug. He piled a couple of sugar-coated doughnuts onto a plate and set it in front of him.

"You mean her apple pie?"

"Not her pies, although her recipe is excellent." He raised his fingertips to his mouth and loudly kissed them. "I mean Mariah herself. Business has really picked up since she came to work for me. Those fellows aren't interested in my moose pot roast with cranberry sauce, either.''

This was something Christian hadn't considered. Mariah had been living in Hard Luck for the better part of a year and had barely caused any reaction among the men in town. He'd never understood it. Many a time he'd have given his eyeteeth for one of his pilots to sweep her off her feet—and out from under his. It hadn't happened. Nor did he understand what was so different now.

"Who?" he demanded. Damn it, he wasn't about to let a bunch of lovesick pilots pester her! Christian didn't linger on the contradictions between his attitude today and that of two months ago. If his men wanted to come in and eat at Ben's, then fine, but anything else and they'd answer to him. After all, he'd been responsible for bringing her to Alaska; he was responsible for ensuring her safety and well-being while she was here. That was why he had to protect her from the pilots. He didn't feel completely convinced there wasn't anything going on between her and Duke, either. She claimed there wasn't, but from the pilot's behavior earlier, Christian was beginning to think otherwise. Duke might well be smitten. Mariah needed the gentle guidance of an older brother, a good friend. Someone like himself.

"Bill Landgrin for one," Ben answered.

The name caught Christian's attention immediately. The pipeline worker was a known troublemaker. Generally Christian was able to get along with just about everyone, but Bill rubbed him the wrong way. He frowned, disliking the thought of Mariah having anything to do with the likes of Bill.

"Who else?"

"Ralph asked her out," Ben murmured, dropping his voice. He glanced over his shoulder to make sure Mariah wasn't listening in on their conversation.

"Ralph Ferris?" One of Christian's own pilots. He felt not only betrayed but puzzled. Ralph had seen Mariah on a daily basis for a whole year. If he'd been interested, he could have asked her out before this. Why he'd pursue her now didn't make sense, especially if Duke had set his sights on her. *None* of this made sense.

"You don't look pleased."

"I'm not," Christian admitted. Unfortunately he wasn't in a position to do anything about it.

"Not that you have a say in the matter." Ben echoed his own thoughts, again keeping his voice low.

Christian met Ben's gaze evenly. They'd been friends for a lot of years. Good friends. Frankly Christian didn't like the idea of a woman standing between them, and he stated his feelings.

"I want her back."

Ben laughed.

It wasn't the reaction Christian had expected, to say the least.

Still grinning, Ben said, "I knew that the minute you walked in here. It might come as a surprise, old friend, but I haven't got her tied to the stove back there. Mariah's free to leave or stay, whichever she decides."

"Fine, just as long as you know where I—where *we* stand," he amended, adding Sawyer and Charles to the equation.

"To my way of thinking, you shouldn't have let her go in the first place," Ben said. He frowned, giving the impression that he didn't understand how the O'Hallorans had been so foolish.

Christian didn't have an answer.

MARIAH WAS ELBOW-DEEP in flour as she strained to hear the conversation taking place between Christian and Ben. She didn't mean to snoop—well, to be honest, she did. She wanted to hear what Christian was saying and strained to make out every word. She couldn't help wanting to know if he missed her, or if he'd given her absence so much as a passing thought.

Ben's voice drifted into the kitchen far more clearly than Christian's. She heard the café owner tell Christian about Bill Landgrin's interest in her and smiled to herself. Not that she'd ever seriously consider dating Bill. That would be asking for trouble. The word got around fast about Bill and his roving hands. Besides, there was only one man who interested Mariah, and he was sitting in this very café, whispering about her.

The phone rang, and she heard Ben amble over to the telephone next to the cash register. A moment later, the cook shouted, "Mariah, it's long-distance for you."

Mariah quickly dusted the flour from her hands and reached for the extension on the kitchen wall. "This is Mariah," she said into the mouthpiece.

Once he was sure she'd picked up the phone, Ben replaced the receiver.

"Mariah, it's Tracy. What the hell happened?"

"Happened?" Her friend sounded upset.

"I called Midnight Sons, and Sawyer said you no longer worked there and suggested I contact you at the Hard Luck Café."

"I quit," Mariah explained simply.

Tracy exhaled a sharp breath. "What did Christian do *this* time?"

Mariah loved the way her friend immediately assumed Christian was the one to blame. This was one of Tracy's most endearing traits—she was loyal to a fault.

"What makes you think Christian did anything?"

"I know the man. He's done everything in his power to make your life miserable."

"That's not true." Mariah found herself wanting to defend Christian. "I'd been with Midnight Sons a year, and it seemed time to move on, that's all."

"You didn't mention it while we were in Anchorage."

"I—I didn't decide until after I returned."

"Something happened." Tracy wasn't about to accept such a weak explanation. "You didn't come up with this idea on the spur of the moment. I know you far too well to believe that. Christian O'Halloran drove you to it."

"No one drove me to anything," Mariah insisted. "I work with Ben now." She didn't mention that she wasn't sure Ben could afford to keep her much longer. Her pies were selling as fast as she could bake them, but her waitressing skills left a lot to be desired.

Thus far, Ben had been exceedingly patient with her, but she'd already broken two coffeepots. She'd offered to have him deduct the cost from her paycheck, but he'd declined.

To Mariah's own disappointment, she had to acknowledge that she lacked the skills to be a waitress. She confused orders and had a tendency not to look where she was going. Only this morning, she'd dumped a plate of poached eggs on Keith Campbell's lap. It hadn't been intentional of course, but Keith had been annoyed, to put it mildly.

Mariah had tried to apologize, but Keith hadn't given her a chance. He'd stomped out. Ben didn't seem distressed to lose Keith as a customer, either, saying he'd

just as soon do without Keith's business. No big loss,
Ben assured her.

"I had to leave Midnight Sons," Mariah admitted
miserably.

"I thought as much," Tracy said in a soothing voice.
"Do you want me to file a lawsuit against them?"

"On what grounds?" Mariah demanded. The
O'Hallorans had been good to her. They'd deeded her
twenty acres of their own land, plus given her the cabin.
In a way she felt they'd saved her by granting her the
means to escape her family's dominance.

"I'm sure we could come up with something," Tracy
said.

Tracy was by nature confrontational, which made her
a good attorney. But that was also the reason for her
problem with Duke, Mariah realized. The pilot took
delight in saying outlandish things just to rile Tracy, and
it worked every time.

"I'd never sue the O'Hallorans," Mariah stressed,
wanting to make that clear.

"Christian's at the root of this, and I—" Tracy continued.

"Tracy," Mariah said, cutting off her friend, "listen.
I'm perfectly happy. Midnight Sons will survive without me." The real question was whether she'd survive
without them—or without one of them, anyway. But for
pride's sake she couldn't admit that, not even to her
friend.

They talked for a few more minutes, with Mariah
struggling to convince Tracy she was happy and at the
same time convince herself.

Working for Ben was what she wanted. She said it
over and over, and once Tracy was satisfied that Ma-

riah had been the one to initiate the change, she was less
concerned.

"Promise you'll contact me if you need anything?"
Tracy asked. "I'll do anything I can to help you, as a
friend and as an attorney."

Mariah promised, but she couldn't imagine why she'd
ever need an attorney.

BETHANY STOOD at the front of the classroom and
looked down the evenly spaced rows of empty desks. In
a matter of days those same desks would again be filled
with Hard Luck's children.

A sense of pride, mingled with responsibility, suddenly overwhelmed her. She loved her job. She loved
Alaska. Although she'd never asked Ben what had
drawn him to the tiny Arctic community, she thought she
understood. The beauty of this place often stole her
breath. She defied anyone to look over the tundra in full
bloom, to smell the scent of fresh, clean air mingled with
spruce and wildflowers, and not understand.

Yes, there was also the challenge of winter, the difficulty of living week upon week in almost total darkness
and subzero temperatures. Not everyone was suited to
this life.

Spring brought with it far more than daylight and
budding flowers, she mused. With the end of winter
came a sense of—she wasn't sure just what to call it—
accomplishment, she decided. Bethany remembered experiencing this phenomenon the previous spring. She'd
realized that she'd survived the dark and the cold of
winter. She'd stood in the sun, soaking up the light, her
arm stretched high above her head toward the bright
blue sky. With that moment came a feeling of power. In
those few special moments, she realized that with love,

with determination, with the force of her own inner strength, there wasn't anything she couldn't accomplish. The feeling had never left her.

Bethany smiled, thinking of Ben, and how coming to find him, meeting this man who'd given her life, had changed her. She was grateful to him in more ways than she could express. Without Ben she'd never have met Mitch and Chrissie.

"My, my, but you're looking thoughtful."

Mitch stood in the classroom doorway, his arms crossed. Tall and muscular, he was dressed in his Department of the Interior uniform. Her heart swelled with pride and love at the sight of her husband.

"I was just thinking about Ben," Bethany said.

"You're worried about him, aren't you?"

It would be useless to deny it. "I guess I am. He just didn't look good the other night."

"Sweetheart, you woke him out of a sound sleep."

"I know." Ben had been thrilled with the news of her pregnancy, and they'd chatted and laughed for an hour before she'd headed home.

Not until she dressed for bed that night did she give the matter of her visit a second thought. Something wasn't right with Ben, but she couldn't put her finger on it.

"I came to take you to lunch," Mitch told her, "since Chrissie's playing at Susan's. You'll be able to see for yourself that Ben's as cantankerous as always."

"Lunch," Bethany said, grinning. "You always did know the way to my heart."

CHRISTIAN DIDN'T THINK he could avoid being obvious when he stopped in at the Hard Luck Café for dinner that evening. The special, barbecued elk ribs, was cer-

tainly not his favorite meal. Nor was he keen on having
half of Hard Luck watch him make a fool of himself.
But he had no choice. Somehow, some way, he needed
to convince Mariah to return to Midnight Sons.

His day hadn't gone well. Sawyer was on his back
about hiring a replacement. The phone had kept them
hopping all afternoon. The pilots were complaining.
Nothing seemed right. Sometimes Christian forgot what
an ill-tempered bunch they could be.

He thought wryly that even when Mariah *wasn't* at the
office, she managed to make his life miserable.

When he entered the café, Christian was shocked by
how busy it was. The place was packed. Every seat at the
counter was taken and all the tables were occupied. The
last empty spot in the entire restaurant was tucked away
in the far corner. Considering himself fortunate, Christian grabbed that before someone else could take it.

"I'll be with you in a minute," Mariah said as she
rushed past Christian, pen and pad in hand. She'd gone
two or three steps before she realized who it was. Turning back, she offered him a brief but tired smile. "Hello,
Christian."

"Mariah." For an instant he had to stop himself from
rising out of his chair to help her. The temptation was so
strong he literally had to hold on to the table. She didn't
belong here, doing this job. She should be with him, not
a roomful of other men.

"Mariah, isn't my order up yet?"

"Mariah, I need more coffee."

"Mariah, did you forget my apple pie?"

When Christian couldn't bear to listen any longer, he
left the table, hurried past her and directly into the
kitchen, where he found Ben filling dinner plates as fast
as he could.

"Don't you hear what's going on out there?" he demanded.

"Sure I do," Ben said, chuckling. "I'm hearing the clang of that cash register. Didn't I tell you Mariah's been a real boon to my sales?"

"They're not giving her a moment's peace!" Christian clenched his fists at his sides.

"Ben, I need—" Mariah flew into the kitchen and stopped dead in her tracks when she found Christian standing there. "More rolls," she finished weakly.

"I want to talk to you," Christian said, holding her captive with his stare.

"I can't." She looked over her shoulder. "I've got a roomful of hungry people all wanting their food right this minute." Her harried gaze darted past him to the counter, where Ben had placed the rolls. "I'm sorry, Christian, but I just can't."

"You're running yourself ragged," he said in a tone few would ignore. His patience was gone. He'd make her an offer she couldn't refuse. He wanted her out of this café, and he didn't care what it cost him.

"She can't talk now." It was Ben who answered on her behalf. "You seem to forget Mariah works for me now. If you have anything to say to her, you'll have to do it on *her* time, not mine."

"Fine," Christian said, gritting his teeth with frustration. "I'll walk you home."

"That . . . that won't work, either," Mariah said, biting her lower lip. "Ralph already asked if he could walk me home, and I told him he could."

"Ralph," Christian repeated bitterly. Well, he'd have something to say about that. The man was not only his employee but a personal friend. Or used to be.

Christian's mood didn't improve during his meal. He watched as Mariah fluttered from one table to another, growing more harried every minute. It gave him no pleasure to realize he hadn't underestimated her skills. Mariah made mistake after mistake, but what amazed him was that not a single customer complained. Half the time the men didn't even bother to correct her.

If she gave someone the wrong order she never knew it; people ate what they were served or traded with someone else.

Once he'd finished dishing up the meals, Ben positioned himself in front of the cash register and gleefully collected money. He grinned from ear to ear each time the register rang.

The only person in the entire restaurant who didn't seem happy was Christian. He'd planned to wait it out, convince Ralph to let him walk Mariah home, but after an hour he couldn't sit idle any longer.

His mood soured as the men openly flirted with her. It infuriated him when they told her how pretty she looked and how her presence brightened the whole place. It was all rubbish, and yet Mariah ate it up as quickly as they downed her apple pie.

He paid his tab and left wearing a scowl.

When he arrived home, his mood still hadn't improved. He turned on the television for a while. Thanks to the satellite dish, he had a large number of choices. But he surfed from channel to channel, unable to find a program that held his interest.

Disgusted with himself, he turned off the set and reached for the novel he'd started the week before. He read ten pages and couldn't remember a single word. Slamming the book closed, he began to pace. Soon he found himself studying the clock.

Ben closed shop around eight. He figured with cleanup and all, it would take an hour or so before Ralph escorted Mariah to her cabin. His jaw tightened at the thought, but Christian knew he had no claim on her time. Nor did he want one, he tried to convince himself.

It was just that he felt responsible for Mariah, he told himself not for the first time. Yeah, responsible, the way a man might feel toward his little sister. She needed a guiding hand, someone to advise her and caution her.

He'd definitely cleared that up in his own mind. He felt immeasurably better.

Although he'd made a point of letting her know he wanted to talk to her, he wasn't entirely sure what he was going to say. He was walking a fine line here, and he knew it. If he pressured her, she'd resist.

What he hoped would happen was that she'd openly admit she missed Midnight Sons. At that point, Christian would be free to suggest she return. But he could see this wasn't likely without some concessions on his part. If only he could figure out exactly what they should be!

Christian bided his time, counted off the minutes, then walked out of the house. He stood on his front porch and stared across the street at his brother's place.

Scott and Eagle Catcher were playing in the front yard. The boy was tossing a stick, and with boundless energy the husky was retrieving it. Susan was playing dolls with Chrissie Harris on the porch steps.

The reflection of the television screen showed in the window, and Christian assumed Sawyer and Abbey were cuddled up in front of it watching the news.

A year. In an amazingly short time his brother had become completely domesticated. Christian was pleased for him, but he wanted none of this for himself. His life was just the way he liked it. One thing was certain: he didn't want a woman trying to change him, messing with his individuality. He'd leave this marriage-and-family stuff to his two older brothers.

He sighed as he walked down the porch steps and buried his hands in his pockets. He sincerely hoped Charles and Sawyer appreciated what he was about to do. If he was successful, they'd have their secretary back. If not, well, he'd deal with that after he'd talked to Mariah.

"Where you headed, Uncle Christian?" Scott asked, running to catch up with him. Eagle Catcher was like a shadow at his side.

"For a walk." He hoped the brevity of his response would give Scott the hint.

"Someone's playing cowboys and Indians," Scott said conversationally.

"Really?"

"Yup, they're sending signals." Scott stopped, hands on his hips. "They're not doing it right, though. Look." He pointed toward the cabins where Mariah lived. "See all that smoke?"

"Smoke?"

Christian whirled around, and sure enough, a trail of dark smoke spiraled upward. His heart kicked into gear. "That's no Indian sending smoke signals," he shouted. "That's a fire!"

CHAPTER SIX

FIRE. MARIAH'S HEART hammered against her rib cage as she fought her overwhelming panic.

At first she tried to battle down the flames, but her puny efforts only seemed to make matters worse. The blaze swished out from the piping that led from her stove, and licked ravenously at the old wood.

Soon the room was engulfed in smoke. Mariah choked and coughed, struggling to breathe. Grabbing what clothes she could, she staggered outside.

Air. Beautiful clean air filled her lungs. She sucked in a deep breath and immediately had a coughing fit. With no time to spare, she dragged in another lungful, then hurried back into the burning cabin for her purse and passport.

Blinded by the smoke, she fumbled about helplessly, seeking her important papers, plus the most precious item she owned, the little jade bear. She could *not* lose that to the fire. All at once her mind wouldn't function properly. Where, oh where, had she set her purse? And the bear—wasn't it on her nightstand?

"Mariah."

Someone yelled her name, but it sounded as if it had come from a great distance. She felt herself weakening, needing desperately to breathe. The smoke dulled her senses, but she refused to give up, refused to leave until she'd found the jade and her purse.

"Mariah!" Whoever sought her was much closer now. Her name came to her, sounding frantic and fearful.

"Here." How pitifully weak she felt. Not until she recognized a pair of men's shoes did she realize that she was on the floor.

"Dear God."

Strong arms scooped her up and carried her out the door.

Air again. Beautiful, clean air.

She breathed in deeply, coughed again and staggered back toward the house.

"Mariah, are you crazy?" Christian stopped her by circling his arms about her waist. "You can't go back."

"But—"

"Nothing in there is worth dying for, damn it!"

He didn't understand, didn't realize what she was after, so she fought him, using every ounce of strength she possessed. She tugged and pulled but made no headway against his superior strength.

"Mariah," he said, turning her around. "Stop!" His fingers dug unmercifully into her shoulders. The fire hissed and spit, the heat so fierce it was suffocating.

"My purse, the bear..."

"Bear? What bear?"

In the distance Mariah heard the fire siren, piercing the evening with its urgency, screaming tragedy to the entire town.

"My purse and your gift—I need them." She'd lost everything, but her mind focused on the two things she valued most. She was thinking less and less clearly. So little made sense.

"You mean to tell me you risked your fool neck over your *purse?*" Christian shouted.

She jerked her elbows from side to side, futilely seeking release. "Let me go!"

"Not on your life," he said, none too gently. "Not on your life."

The bright yellow fire truck screeched to a stop in front of the burning cabin. Five or six men moved with amazing agility to free the hose. Their figures blurred as they worked together.

Mariah recognized Sawyer and Mitch Harris and Marvin Gold, who were all members of the volunteer fire department. She wanted to shout to them to hurry, but even as the words worked their way up her throat, she knew it was too late. All was lost—her home and everything inside it. No hope remained.

With his arm wrapped protectively around her, Christian drew her away from her cabin, which was by now fully engulfed in flames. A chill came over her as she stood by and silently watched the fire swallow up everything she owned, every possession she owned, save an armful of clothes she'd managed to snatch.

A breathless Dotty Livengood arrived, having raced from her home. "Is Mariah all right?" She directed the question at Christian.

"I don't know."

"Let me check her."

"Mariah." Before Dotty reached her, Christian placed his hands on her shoulders and turned her to face him. "Were you burned?"

Mariah saw his lips move and heard the words, but it was as though he was standing on the other side of a glass wall. Nothing seemed to touch her, to penetrate her confusion and loss. The question took several moments to register. Was she hurt? Had she been burned? She felt no pain, not physical at least. Only loss, deep and personal loss.

"Her hands." This comment came from Christian, and it seemed to her, even from this emotional distance, that he was angry, frustrated. "It looks like she blistered her fingers."

"She must have tried to put out the fire herself." Dotty's gentle voice soothed her.

"I can't believe what she just did," Christian muttered. "I had to drag her out of the house. She was after her purse and some silly figurine I gave her. She risked her damn-fool neck for a forty-dollar piece of jade." His anger spilled out of him like water hissing against a hot burner.

"Christian." It was Dotty again, her voice forceful. "Calm down."

"I can't," he shouted. "Do you realize she could have *died* in there? If I hadn't arrived when I did, no one would've been able to save her. We barely got out in time."

"Take several deep breaths," Dotty instructed calmly. "You've both had a fright, but you're safe now. Everything's going to be fine."

"Her purse and a figurine! She was willing to die trying to save them!" The rage in Christian seemed to intensify as the other men dealt with the fire. He started to pace, his steps abrupt and awkward as he attempted to manage his anger.

Mariah was only now beginning to comprehend what had happened. She wasn't sure how the fire had started; all she knew was that she'd lit her stove, trying to chase away the chill. It'd been weeks since she'd lit the thing, and there must have been something in the chimney, because the next thing she knew the pipe started to glow.

The dry cabin wall behind it caught fire and then, half a minute later, the curtains. The flames roared across the room so quickly, they'd been impossible to stop.

"Take her over to the clinic," Dotty instructed Christian. "I'll tend to those burns right away."

Others started to arrive, children and adults alike. Their eyes filled with sympathy and fear.

"Go," Dotty told Christian.

He guided Mariah away from the gathering crowd. She looked back only once at what had been her home.

Dotty arrived a little later. "They weren't able to save anything," she said sadly.

"It would've been impossible," Christian said. He couldn't seem to stand still. And Mariah could barely move; she didn't have the strength. It felt as though someone had sucked the very life from her. It was an effort just keeping her head up.

"Mariah," Dotty said in a gentle voice, "you've had quite a shock."

Christian paced the clinic. "She was on the floor when I found her," he said forcefully. "If I'd arrived a minute later I might never have reached her. She came so close to dying in the fire."

"Christian, you've had a scare, too."

"The woman hasn't got a brain in her head. Just how important can a purse be?" With rough, angry movements, he rubbed the back of his neck. "She shouldn't even have been *living* in that cabin. The place is a firetrap! But she was so damn stubborn, insisting this was where she had to stay—"

"Christian!"

"She should go back to Seattle!" he exploded. "Hell, I'll personally pay for her ticket. At least there she won't be dealing with fires and a bunch of women-hungry men making demands on her.''

She should be back in Seattle. The words penetrated the haze in Mariah's mind, and a sob erupted from deep within her throat. Christian had never made a secret of how he felt about her, but the fact that he could be so cruel now, when she'd lost everything, was more than she could bear.

"Christian O'Halloran, what a perfectly rotten thing to say!" Dotty snapped. "I think it would be best if you left. The last thing Mariah needs now is you haranguing her.''

Mariah watched Christian stomp out of the health clinic.

Leaning her head against the wall, she sighed and closed her eyes. Tears were close to the surface, but she held them at bay, concentrating, instead, on the pain in her hands. They had started to throb, and she was grateful when Dotty returned.

Soon Dotty had tended to her burns and bandaged her hands. Shortly after that, Abbey and Lanni O'Halloran stopped by with Karen Caldwell and Bethany Harris to check on her.

"Are you okay?" Abbey asked, sitting next to Mariah and placing an arm around her shoulders.

"I'm fine," Mariah assured her friends. But she wasn't. The sense of devastation hit her again, bringing fresh tears. Everything she'd worked for in the past year was lost. The man she secretly loved was furious with her. Now her hands were burned and bandaged and she was unable to work. She had no home, no place to live.

"If I was smart, I'd do what Christian said," she mumbled, forcing herself to smile.

"What did Christian say?" Bethany asked, glancing at Dotty.

"He suggested she return to Seattle," the nurse answered, her lips pinched disapprovingly. "Someone needs to have a talk with that young man."

"He said *what?*" Lanni demanded, outraged.

"How dare he!" This came from Karen.

The atmosphere in the room crackled with indignation.

"Just a moment," Abbey said, stroking Mariah's back. "Let's not be so quick to condemn him. I had a chance to talk to him just now, and you know what? I've never seen Christian so upset."

With me, Mariah added silently.

"He's had the scare of a lifetime. Think about it. Christian almost lost Mariah, and I don't think he could handle that."

"Then why would he say something so terrible to her, especially now?" Lanni asked, her eyes flashing at the insult.

"In my experience, a man will express what he fears most, rather than let it sneak up on him. Women do the same thing, but not as often."

"You're making excuses for him," Bethany said, sounding none too pleased with the youngest O'Halloran.

"No," Abbey insisted softly. "I think he'll be back to apologize to Mariah the minute he realizes what he said. Christian no more wants Mariah to move back to Seattle than he wants to live there himself."

"And if he doesn't apologize, then I know a number of women who'll be more than happy to assist him in realizing his mistake," Karen said meaningfully.

Dotty chuckled softly. "You know, I almost feel sorry for that boy."

"Now listen, Mariah, we've got this all figured out," Abbey assured her, again with a gentle firmness.

"Right." Karen stood in the center of the room, arms akimbo. "You're going to need someplace to live until you rebuild. I'm sure that with all the new construction in town, you could find someone to do it quickly."

"Rebuild. Yes. I—I don't know what I'm going to do," she whispered, grateful for her friends. Her mind remained confused, her confidence in the future badly shaken.

"You don't need to worry about that," Karen continued. "You're going to come and live with Matt and me at the lodge."

"The lodge." Mariah realized she must sound like an echo, but making decisions, even simple ones, was beyond her.

"We're going to take care of everything," Abbey promised. Somehow Mariah doubted that anyone could help her repair the mess she'd made of her life. It was too late for that.

"ARE YOU GOING to the Labor Day community dance?" Ben asked Christian when he arrived for breakfast a couple of days after the fire.

"The dance?" Hard Luck routinely celebrated Labor Day with a festive get-together. Because of all the problems at the office and the chaos following the fire, Christian hadn't given the matter more than a fleeting thought. "I guess," he said with little enthusiasm. He attended every Labor Day affair and didn't expect this year to be any different.

"Will you be taking Mariah?"

Christian noticed that Ben had saved that for the punch line. At the sound of Mariah's name, it was all Christian could do to keep from clenching his fists.

Every time he thought about the fire, he became so angry he couldn't think straight. The damn-fool woman had nearly lost her life! A chill ran down his spine again at the realization. He averted his gaze, not wanting Ben to know how intensely all this had affected him.

"Uh, how's she doing?" Christian cut the sour-dough hotcakes with his fork.

"I hear she's staying at the lodge."

Christian nodded; he'd already learned that much.

"With her hands all bandaged up, she can't work. She felt real bad about that," Ben added, "but I've been running this café on my own close to twenty years now. I assured her I could manage for however long it takes her hands to heal."

"Was she badly burned?"

"Nah. Dotty seems to think she'll be back good as new in a week or so."

Christian was relieved to hear it.

"I understand you single-handedly riled every woman in town." Ben chuckled as he walked to the other end of the counter, where Duke and Ralph were finishing breakfast, and refreshed their coffee.

"So it seems," Christian muttered. He wasn't proud of his outburst, but he'd been so coldly furious with Mariah that he couldn't have suppressed the words if he'd tried. At the time, he'd meant every one. He'd never been more frightened in his life. Only last night, he'd awakened in a cold sweat, trembling. He'd dreamed about the fire, that he'd gone into the house and hadn't been able to find Mariah. For a long time after he woke up, his heart continued to race. It was useless to try to sleep again, so before dawn, he'd dressed and gone to the burned-out cabin. He'd stood there until the sun rose, giving incoherent thanks that Mariah had been spared. *"She's safe."* He'd repeated it over and over—but couldn't quite forget that she'd almost died.

"What are you going to do now?" Ben asked.

"What *can* I do? Apologize, I guess," Christian muttered. He glanced over at the two pilots, feeling like a fool. As it was, his own brother had no use for him. Sawyer had yet to forgive him for losing their secretary, and the situation hadn't improved when he hadn't immediately hired another. Now, to make matters even worse, he seemed to be blaming Christian for the danger to Mariah, for letting her stay in the cabin. *Letting* her stay!

"Good." Ben sighed as though the issue of Christian's apology had been weighing heavily on his mind.

After paying his tab, Christian hurried to the office. Sawyer was busy on the phone and left him to deal with the pilots and their assignments for the day. The usual dissatisfaction broke out, but he dealt with it, if rather more ruthlessly than usual.

During a midmorning lull, Christian slipped out and made his way to the lodge to speak to Mariah. On the way, he formulated what he wanted to say. He was so intent on putting his apology together that he didn't notice she was sitting on the front-porch swing.

"Karen and Matt are gone for the morning," she announced as he began to climb the porch steps.

Christian paused, one foot on the ground and the other on the first stair. His gaze was immediately drawn to the bandages on her hands and then to the sadness in her eyes. The need to comfort her was strong, but he knew she didn't want anything to do with him now. Personally he didn't blame her.

Mariah's hair was drawn away from her face, and she wore a simple light green summer dress that suited her perfectly. He didn't recognize it and wondered if one of the woman in town had lent it to her. No matter; she'd never looked lovelier.

"I didn't come to see Karen or Matt," he said, finishing the climb.

It was unseasonably warm for late August, despite some cool days the week before. The swing, a recent addition to the lodge, swayed ever so gently in the breeze. He could hear bird song in the distance. The sun splashed over her shoulders, glinting off her red hair, adding an aura of cheerfulness he knew was false.

He found it difficult to pull his gaze from hers. Her look was blank, neither welcoming nor unwelcoming. She'd been the same way the night of the fire, lost and confused.

"I came to apologize for what I said," he blurted. He might as well deal with the unpleasantness right away. "I didn't mean it. The last thing I want you to do is leave Alaska."

"But you wouldn't object if I found my way out of Hard Luck." Her voice was as dispassionate as her eyes.

"No, that's not what I meant. I don't want you to leave Hard Luck." She was making this damned difficult, but then, he suspected he deserved it.

"Here," he muttered, digging inside his jacket pocket. He fished out her jade bear. It had taken no small effort to find the figurine in the charred rubble, and unfortunately he'd been unable to recover her purse. He'd spent hours yesterday morning, once the sun had risen, sifting through the ashes and debris.

Mariah's eyes lit up. "You found my bear!" It was the first emotion she'd shown. Her lower lip trembled, and he realized she was struggling to hold back tears. She gripped the figurine tightly, clasping it to her breast. "Thank you, Christian."

He shrugged, making light of the accomplishment. "It was nothing."

Her beautiful brown eyes continued to hold his. Annoyed, Christian looked away. Not because he didn't find her attractive—he did, more so each time he saw her—but because she reminded him of what he'd been trying to forget ever since he'd kissed her. He didn't want to see her eyes like this, wide and beguiling. He couldn't resist their luminous beauty or her enticing mouth or soft, pale skin. If he looked at her, he'd want to kiss her again.

He remembered when Charles had first learned about Lanni's relationship to Catherine Fletcher and how he'd avoided looking at her. But this was different, he told himself. This was Mariah, and his feelings toward her were crystal clear. She needed someone—an older-brother kind of someone—to help her. A friend to steer her in the right direction. Christian wasn't like his brothers. No, sir. Charles and Sawyer wore their hearts on their sleeves. Not Christian. Sure, he'd kissed Mariah, but that had been a . . . a fluke.

Yet even now, after all this time, he could remember the way she'd felt, the way her mouth had tasted. He'd done everything he could to push that memory to the farthest reaches of his mind, but to no avail.

Damn. Maybe, just maybe, he was like his brothers.

Without invitation he sat down on the swing next to her. It seemed important that she realize how sincere his apology was. "I'm sorry—I don't know what came over me the night of the fire," he muttered, knowing that was no excuse, but he had none better to offer. "It's just that you could have died." His jaw tightened as a surge of anger threatened to take control of him all over again. "If you decide you never want to speak to me because of the things I said, I wouldn't blame you. But I'm hoping you won't do that."

He couldn't believe exactly what he *was* hoping. The urge, the need to kiss her, was back. And it was even more powerful than before.

"I understand, Christian."

"You do?"

"All is forgiven." She smiled, as if amused by the melodramatic words. "You were angry. Upset."

His heart felt lighter. She smiled sweetly at him, and he noted once more that, while she didn't possess the striking beauty of Allison Reynolds, Mariah's loveliness went much deeper. Was so much more *real*.

He stared at her mouth, soft and moist. He recalled how her lips had melted beneath his and how . . .

He cleared his throat and glanced quickly away.

"Thank you for finding the jade piece for me."

"It was the least I could do." He shrugged, tried to grin, but his heart pounded like a lovelorn teenager's.

"Mariah." He whispered her name before he drew her into his arms. She seemed to realize what he was asking of her; she leaned toward him. Their mouths came together with an urgency he'd never experienced.

Christian's breathing was labored. Their previous kisses had been tentative exchanges, brief encounters. No longer. He thrust his tongue into her mouth and growled at her eager response. His hands stroked her slender back.

A noise sounded in the background, and with great reluctance, Christian broke off the kiss. A truck barreled down the dirt road, leaving a trail of dust in its wake.

If he was going to kiss Mariah, Christian decided, he didn't want the entire town looking on.

"Ben misses you," he whispered, hardly able to find his voice. He dared not dwell on how wonderful it was to kiss her, and how difficult it was to keep from kissing her again.

Mariah lowered her lashes and smiled. "I can't imagine why. I'm an even worse waitress than I was a secretary."

"That's not true." The irony of the situation didn't escape him; here he was defending her, when only a few months—weeks!—earlier he'd been the one listing her shortcomings.

"Well, it's a moot point now." Her eyes dulled—with sadness, regret, worry, he wasn't sure which.

"You'll be back in no time." What he hoped, though, was that she'd be back at Midnight Sons. Another truck sped past. Christian had no idea the road in front of the lodge was so damned busy. He checked his watch. Sawyer would be on his case if he stayed any longer. He thought of mentioning that he'd like her back in the office, but he didn't want to rush her. And he didn't want her thinking that kiss had anything to do with work. Besides, he'd already swallowed one serving of crow; he wasn't eager to down another quite so soon. He'd ease into the topic, be sure she understood how much they missed her, how much *he* missed her, and let it go from there.

"I have to go," he said, hoping his voice conveyed his reluctance.

"I know. Thanks for finding the bear for me and for stopping by."

On impulse, he leaned forward and gently pressed his lips to hers. It would've been easy to let the kiss develop into something more than a farewell gesture, but he forced himself to make it just that.

His step was almost jaunty as he hurried back to the office. When he walked in the door, Sawyer cast him a disgruntled look.

"What took you so long?" he muttered, but Christian supposed that his brother didn't actually expect him to answer.

He picked up his phone messages and sat down at his desk to return the calls. His hand was on the telephone receiver when his brother spoke again.

"I hate to be a pest about this," Sawyer said, "but just when the hell can we expect another secretary?"

"Soon." He knew the minute he said the word that he'd used it one time too many.

"You've been saying that ever since Mariah left," Sawyer said impatiently. "Either hire someone else, or I will."

Christian didn't take kindly to ultimatums. "Now listen here, Sawyer. I've put up with about as much of this as I'm going to."

"You! Seems to me you haven't done a damn thing to find Mariah's replacement." He glared at him from across the office. "I'm beginning to think you don't *intend* to hire anyone else."

"I don't."

Sawyer's jaw fell open. "Why the hell not?"

"Because I'm going to convince Mariah to come back."

"I already tried that," Sawyer told him, sighing wearily.

"But I caused the problem, not you."

Sawyer snorted softly. "You won't hear me coming to your defense on that one."

"I planned to say something to her this morning, but—"

"So that's where you were!" Sawyer's look revealed his curiosity.

"Yeah. I apologized and she accepted my apology." He paused. "Ben reminded me about the Labor Day dance, and I think I'll ask Mariah. You know, get back into her good graces." He had an ulterior motive, as well. From now on, Christian wanted every man in town to stay away from her. By escorting her to the dance he was sending a silent message. Mariah was off-limits. Out-of-bounds.

Sawyer brightened. "Ask Mariah to the dance—now that's a good idea. Wine and dine her. Women like that sort of thing."

"I thought as much." Christian felt downright smug. Everything was falling neatly into place, just the way it should.

Before long Mariah would be back at Midnight Sons.

Christian didn't want to appear too anxious, so he waited until the following evening to pay Mariah a second visit. He toyed with the idea of bringing her a small gift. Easier said than done. He surveyed the office and saw the latest issue of *Aviation News* on Sawyer's desk. He tucked it under his arm, thinking she'd enjoy reading it. Maybe it would remind her of everything she'd liked about Midnight Sons, get her back in the mood.

Humming cheerfully to himself, he strolled down the hard dirt road. The evening was chilly, and he was glad he'd remembered his sweatshirt. That way, they could sit out on the porch again. With any luck Karen and Matt would be away. He wasn't planning to kiss Mariah, but if the spirit moved them, well . . .

It wasn't until Christian had rounded the corner to the lodge that he noticed Bill Landgrin's truck parked outside. He stopped, frowning, then increased his pace.

He found Mariah sitting on the swing as if she'd been there all along awaiting his return. She looked as pretty as she had yesterday, but happier, more animated.

Bill was leaning casually against the porch rail, his legs crossed. He certainly seemed to have settled in for the evening.

Christian opened the gate and started purposefully up the walkway. Mariah's eyes found his, and he read the welcome in her look. Landgrin twisted his head around; when he saw Christian, he glared.

"What are you doing here?" Landgrin demanded.

"I've come to see Mariah."

"So have I," the pipeline worker said, sounding none too friendly. "You can wait your turn like everyone else."

"It's going to take someone a whole lot bigger than you to get me to leave," Christian informed the other man in deceptively calm tones. He didn't take kindly to Bill moving in on Mariah, and he wanted that understood right now.

"Bill. Christian. Please."

Both men ignored her. They were too busy glowering at each other. By nature, Christian wasn't a violent man, but there were few people who raised his ire as much as Bill.

"You had your chance with Mariah," Bill said.

Christian didn't know what Bill was implying, but he didn't like it. The fact was, he didn't like the other man, period. One thing was certain: he didn't want Bill anywhere near her.

"She worked for you for a whole year!"

"That has nothing to do with this." The point wasn't worth discussing.

"You could've asked her out at any time. You didn't, so she's fair game for the rest of us."

From the corner of his eye, Christian saw Mariah stand up from the swing. "Will you two kindly stop? You're talking about me like... like I'm some kind of hunting trophy. Fair game!"

Christian had seen Mariah in this mood before. "Bill will apologize," he said immediately, pointing at the other man. "I believe you owe the lady an apology."

"Bill!" Mariah shouted. "What do you mean, Bill? What about *you?*"

Shocked, Christian broke eye contact with Bill long enough to glance her way. "Me? What did I do wrong?"

"How much time have you got?" Bill muttered under his breath, snickering.

Christian reverted his attention to Landgrin. "Okay, I'll say what I came to say, then in the interest of fairness, I'll leave."

"I was here first," Bill took pleasure in reminding him.

"Fine." Christian raised both hands in a gesture of peace, the magazine still tucked under his arm. Then he moved forward and handed it to Mariah. "I thought you might like this."

"Thank you," she replied stiffly.

"And..." he said, clearing his throat. This wasn't easy, especially with another man listening in. "I wanted to know if you'd attend the Labor Day dance with me."

"Now just one damn minute," Landgrin blared. "That's the reason *I'm* here."

A slow, satisfied smile unraveled across Christian's face. "I asked first."

"But I was here first!"

"Bill. Christian."

Again they both ignored her.

"She's going with me," Christian said, glancing briefly at Mariah for confirmation.

"Sorry, pal. If anyone's taking Mariah to that dance, it'll be me."

"Not on your life." Christian was willing to eat a whole lot more than crow just to get Bill out of the picture.

"As it happens," Mariah said sternly, "I won't be attending the dance with either of you. Duke Porter asked me two days ago, and I've already agreed to go as his date."

Having said that, she walked past them both and disappeared into the lodge.

CHAPTER SEVEN

DUKE PORTER! Christian didn't like it, not one damn bit. While he was playing it cool, not wanting to appear overeager—because, of course, he wasn't—Duke had gone behind his back and asked Mariah to the dance. Well, didn't that beat all!

However, Christian wasn't *really* angry that Duke had outdone him, he decided; actually he found the whole thing rather amusing. His own pilot had shown him—and Bill—a thing or two.

Mariah weighed heavily on his mind. His possessive attitude toward her had begun to bother him. Duke he didn't mind because—well, because he knew Duke wasn't romantically interested in her. At least that was what Duke had been claiming for months, and Christian finally believed him.

Bill was another story entirely. He gritted his teeth every time he thought about the pipeline worker making a play for Mariah. What irritated him most was that she didn't see through his fast-talking style. Christian credited her with better sense than that.

In the past few weeks, everything had changed between him and Mariah, and Christian didn't fully understand the differences yet.

Often when he was disturbed about something, he'd pull a flying assignment himself. That morning, instead of delegating Duke to carry the mail into Fairbanks,

Christian decided to make the run himself. He left a quick note, hoping Duke wouldn't mind, and headed out early.

The morning was foggy and cold for the end of August. The mist felt cool and refreshing while he was on the ground, but icy crystals formed on the plane's wings as he headed south.

En route, his thoughts were once again filled with Mariah. True, he wanted her back as his secretary, but he didn't dwell on that. His concern centered on the attention other men were giving her. Naturally, he wasn't interested in her himself, but he didn't want to see her make a mistake.

Mariah was sweet and genuine, a bit naive and, frankly, too damn trusting. At times he wondered if she had the sense God gave a goose, and at others he was astonished by her insight and sensitivity.

The woman perplexed him.

He touched down in Fairbanks and collected the mail, then headed straight back to Hard Luck. An hour later, he landed on the gravel runway.

Duke was in the office waiting when Christian returned from unloading the cargo. The pilot glared at him. "You grounded me—again—because Mariah's attending the dance with me, didn't you?" His eyes fairly snapped with anger.

The verbal attack caught Christian by surprise. He finished removing his black rayon jacket with its Midnight Sons logo on the back before he answered.

"No, Duke, of course not! Didn't you find my note?"

"That didn't explain anything. You took my run! You're angry because Mariah is going to the dance with *me*."

"Where's Sawyer?" He wasn't ignoring the outburst, but needed to know where his brother had disappeared. With the office shorthanded, this was not the time for Sawyer to be yakking over coffee with Ben.

"He stepped out for a couple of minutes. He'll be back. Now answer me, damn it."

Christian exhaled forcefully.

"You can't, and we both know why," snarled Duke. "I've been with Midnight Sons for more years than I want to remember. Until now, I've always considered you and Sawyer to be equitable and fair-minded. No longer." He walked over to the desk and picked up a sheet of paper. "As of this moment, you have my notice."

"Your notice?"

"Yeah," Duke said, his look colder than Christian had ever seen it. "I quit." With that, he grabbed his leather jacket and stalked out the door.

No sooner had Duke left than Sawyer walked in. "What's the problem with Duke? He looked as mad as hops."

"He is," Christian said, and slumped down in his chair. "He just quit."

"What?" Sawyer exploded. "Quit? Why? Duke's been with us almost from the beginning."

"I know." Christian propped his elbows on the desk and resisted the urge to bury his face in his hands. Everything he touched lately turned to dust. Because of him, Midnight Sons had lost Mariah, and now he was solely responsible for Duke's leaving.

Sawyer walked over and read Duke's letter. The message was brief and to the point. Christian could picture the pilot sitting at the keyboard, tapping out the letter with one finger, swearing under his breath and getting angrier by the minute.

"What happened?"

Rather than go into a long and complicated explanation, Christian opted for a shorter version of the truth. "He's upset about me taking the mail run this morning." Christian rubbed a weary hand down his face. "Despite what he thinks, I didn't do it to punish him."

"Punish him?" Sawyer sounded more confused than ever.

"Duke seems to think that because he's taking Mariah to the dance, I—"

"What the bloody hell has that got to do with anything?"

"Absolutely nothing," Christian insisted, close to losing his own patience now. "Why should I care if Duke takes Mariah to the Labor Day dance? I needed time to do some thinking, so I decided to make the mail run. How was I to know Duke would consider it a personal affront?"

"I don't believe this." Sawyer walked from one end of the trailer to the other in agitated strides. "We—Midnight Sons—recruited women to Hard Luck well over a year ago, and everything's gone pretty smoothly.

"Some have come and gone, and others have stayed. The town's thriving. There's been construction all summer. New homes are going up. The lodge's repaired and open for business. John and Sally's mobile home is up, and more are ordered. Midnight Sons started all this, and now Midnight Sons is going down the drain—just when we should be doing better than ever! Could someone kindly tell me why?"

"You're exaggerating."

"I don't think so," Sawyer continued, growing more impassioned. "We've had more complaints in the past two weeks than we've had in two years."

Mariah's absence from their office would explain that.

"Duke's quitting, and he isn't the only unhappy pilot we've got. I wouldn't be surprised if Ralph left with him. We might lose Ted, too."

The pilots had been good friends for a lot of years, and Christian suspected his brother was right. This could result in a mass exodus.

"I'll talk to him," he promised. "It's me Duke's upset with, not the business. I'll give him a couple of hours to settle down, then I'll approach him."

Sawyer's icy glare thawed only a little. "So you're going to take care of this?"

"I'll do my best," Christian promised.

SAWYER NEEDED to get out of the office and vent his frustration. He walked to the library, located in the log cabin that had once belonged to his grandfather. Abbey sat behind the desk, busy updating her meticulous files. She looked up and smiled warmly when he walked in.

"My, oh my," she greeted him. "Sure looks like you're having one of those days."

"Duke handed in his notice."

It was almost comical to watch Abbey's expressive eyes fill with shock. "Duke? But why? Something must have happened!"

"Christian." If it wasn't so serious, Sawyer might've laughed over his younger brother's condition. He recognized the symptoms, having experienced them himself a year earlier.

Christian was falling in love.

"What did he do this time?"

Sawyer could see by the look on his wife's face that she was fast losing patience with her brother-in-law.

"He took the mail run himself, grounding Duke. Christian claimed he needed a chance to think, but Duke figured it was a form of punishment because he'd asked Mariah to the dance."

"Was it?"

Sawyer pulled out a chair at the reading table, a recent addition to the library. "I don't know. I don't think so. Christian may not be the most sensitive guy in the world, but he'd never intentionally do anything to upset the pilots or hurt the business."

"You know what's wrong with him, don't you?" Abbey asked.

"I have my suspicions."

Abbey smiled, and for the life of him, Sawyer couldn't take his eyes off her. She grew more beautiful every day, he thought, especially now that she was carrying his baby.

"Christian's in love."

Sawyer chuckled. "Was I this bad?"

"Worse," she said primly, leaving no room for doubt.

"Oh, come on," Sawyer returned. "You know what the real problem is? Christian's the youngest of the family, and—"

"Exactly," Abbey cut in, "and his role models are you and Charles." She shook her head. "The poor guy's so confused he doesn't have a clue how to behave with a woman."

"What's wrong with Charles and me?" Sawyer demanded.

"You mean I have to explain it?" Abbey rolled her eyes. "Charles was willing to let Lanni walk out of his life—all because of an old family feud. And you, my fine husband, offered me one of the most insulting marriage proposals any woman's ever likely to receive.''

"I was desperate," he said quickly.

"My point exactly. With such pathetic examples, it's no wonder Christian can't decipher his feelings.''

"I might not have said all the fancy words women like to read in those books," he said, gesturing toward the romance section in the fiction department, "but I got my message across, didn't I?''

Her faced softened and she grinned, patting her rounded stomach. "You most certainly did.''

Sawyer had known he loved Abbey and her children a year ago, but his feelings then couldn't compare with their intensity now. In retrospect, his life had been empty and shallow before he'd met Abbey. Her love gave him a sense of purpose, a reason to get up in the morning. Abbey and the children were his incentive to be the best husband and father—the best *man*—he could.

"Maybe we should...help Christian," Abbey suggested. "Subtly, of course. He'll resist any open attempts to steer him in the right direction.''

"Christian would resent it if we intruded.''

Abbey looked disappointed. "You're sure?''

"It won't do a damn bit of good, sweetheart," Sawyer told her. "My brother's got to figure this out all on his own the same way Charles did.''

"And you!''

"And me," Sawyer agreed with a grin.

Abbey chewed on her lower lip. "It took Charles *weeks*, remember?''

Sawyer wasn't likely to forget. His older brother had walked around town like a wounded bear, snapping at everyone in his vicinity.

"I just wonder..." Sawyer murmured.

"What?"

Sawyer shook his head. "If Midnight Sons will survive Christian's falling in love."

DUKE WAS SITTING glumly on the end of his bed when Christian let himself into the bunkhouse. He glanced up; as soon as he saw who it was, he looked away.

"You got a minute?" Christian asked.

Duke made a show of checking his watch. "I suppose." He stood up and crossed to his locker, pulled out a duffel bag and started stuffing things into it.

"I'd like to talk to you about your leaving Midnight Sons."

"Yeah, well, I didn't think you wanted to chat about the weather."

Duke's back was to him, and Christian was having a hell of a time finding the right words. He was willing enough to apologize, only he wasn't sure what he was supposed to apologize *for*.

"Uh, taking your run this morning," Christian began, broaching the topic tentatively. "I should've explained why I did that. I needed to think something over, and I do that best when I'm in the air." The excuse sounded weak even to his own ears, but he'd swear on his father's grave that he hadn't been punishing Duke for asking Mariah to the dance.

Duke whirled around to face him. "Tell me, Christian, do I look like a bloody secretary?"

The question took him aback. "No. I don't understand why you'd ask that?"

"Well, what do you think I was doing for two and a half hours this morning? Answering the phone, looking for files, running errands."

"You didn't need to do any of that."

"Well, Sawyer couldn't do it all. He was rushing around all morning. What was I supposed to do, ignore the phone? I go in to complain about you taking my flight, and next thing I know I'm talking to some dame in Anchorage. She claims she's a travel agent and insists she's booked all these flights with us. I couldn't find a darn thing in any of the files that says she did or didn't."

"Did her name happen to be Penny Ferguson?"

"Yeah, she's the one," Duke said, narrowing his eyes.

Christian groaned and covered his face. He'd resign, too, if he'd been stuck on the phone with Penny, who was demanding and difficult.

"I apologize," Christian said. "I never intended for you to have to deal with Mrs. Ferguson."

"You mean she's married?" Duke shook his head. "My condolences to Mr. Ferguson. The woman reminded me of that attorney friend of Mariah's."

At the mention of her name, Christian cleared his throat. It was now or never. "Speaking of Mariah..." he began, uncertain where to head from there.

"What's with the two of you, anyway?" Duke asked. The anger had left his eyes, replaced with curiosity.

"Nothing," Christian said quickly, perhaps too quickly.

Duke frowned, then shrugged. "If that's what you say, who am I to argue?" He turned around and stuffed a shirt deep into his duffel bag.

"About your letter of resignation," Christian said, approaching the subject cautiously. "I'm hoping I can get you to reconsider. You're a valuable part of our business—probably one of the best damn pilots in all of Alaska." A little flattery was sure to help, although that statement wasn't far from the truth.

Duke didn't respond.

"I looked over the payroll file and noticed it was well past time for you to get a raise."

Duke faced him again, his interest obviously piqued. "What're you offering?"

In the last year or so, Midnight Sons had been doing good business. Very good. "Twenty percent increase in your base salary."

Duke's eyes widened. "Hot damn. Mariah thought you'd only go for ten." He clamped his mouth shut and flushed.

Christian raised his eyebrows. "You discussed this with Mariah?"

"Yeah," Duke answered in a way that challenged him to make something of it. "She was the one who talked me into staying. If it wasn't for her, I'd have been out of here on the afternoon flight." He shoved his duffel bag into the locker and slammed the door. "You might say I was a bit agitated when I left your office this morning. I stopped off at the lodge, and Mariah and I had a long talk."

Christian would have liked to be a bug on the wall for that.

"She's loyal to you, Christian. Real loyal. The thing is, I'm not sure you deserve it."

At this point, neither was Christian.

MUSIC BLARED from several huge speakers strategically set about the polished hardwood floor. It was Labor Day, and Hard Luck's school gymnasium was as packed as it had been only rarely since the state had built the school during the oil-rich years.

Linen-covered tables arranged against the wall were laden with food left over from the earlier potluck. There were salads of all kinds and desserts to tempt the saints, and a dozen casseroles redolent with onion and garlic and savory herbs. Contributions to the feast had been so plentiful that by nine o'clock, enough food remained to feed everyone a second time.

Mariah had made four apple pies, although Karen had peeled the apples. She was able to do most things for herself, although the bandages tended to frustrate her. But they'd be off soon enough, according to Dotty.

Duke had been a thoughtful, devoted companion all evening, and following the dinner, they'd danced a number of times.

Schoolchildren raced with inexhaustible energy from one end of the room to the other. Several had removed their shoes and slipped and skidded across the slick floor.

So far Mariah hadn't seen Christian, and she was beginning to wonder if he'd make an appearance. And if he did, she wondered if he'd bring another woman to the festivities. Foolishly Mariah had dreamed of seeing Christian here; she'd dreamed that he would take her in his arms, dance with her, kiss her... But that was all fantasy, she reminded herself.

Christian probably wouldn't even show, but Mariah had given up second-guessing her former boss. The kisses they'd exchanged had been incredible, but as far as she could tell they meant nothing to Christian. Afterward, he'd looked repentant and even angry with himself. Except the last time.

Because her feet hurt from new shoes, Mariah sat out the next dance. Duke, however, became involved in an imaginative free-form dance with Angie Hughes.

"Hello, Mariah."

"Christian...hello." He'd snuck up on her. Her heart reacted with an immediate leap of happiness.

"How's the dance going?" he asked, sitting in the empty chair beside her.

"Great." Her pulse reacted as if she'd been caught doing something illegal.

After a few moments of silence, he said, "I understand I owe you a debt of thanks."

Her eyes opened wide in surprise. She couldn't think clearly when he was this close. The light, spicy scent of his after-shave sent her senses reeling. She considered it grossly unfair that he should affect her like this when he clearly didn't return her feelings.

"Duke explained you'd talked him into staying," he continued.

She shrugged, making light of her involvement.

"I want you to know I appreciate it." He hesitated and rubbed his hand down his thigh. "I don't know what it is lately, but I seem to have developed a talent for making enemies."

"That's not true." As always she was prepared to defend him. "It wasn't you Duke was angry with, but Mrs. Ferguson."

He smiled and seemed grateful for her support.

"Have you eaten?" Mariah's mother seemed to think food was a remedy for all problems, social or personal, and Mariah found herself falling back on that familiar solution. "Dotty's salmon casserole is wonderful." She regretted opening her mouth almost immediately. She strongly suspected that women like Allison Reynolds didn't rave about someone's salmon casserole.

"I ate earlier," he said.

It seemed everyone in the room was glancing their way with expressions of anticipation and curiosity. If Christian noticed he didn't comment. It was all Mariah could do not to stand up and beg everyone to ignore them.

"Would you like to dance?"

Mariah couldn't have been more shocked if he'd proposed marriage. *Her dream come true.* "Yes—that would be very nice." She forgot how much her feet hurt; at that moment she would gladly have walked across broken glass for the opportunity to be in Christian's arms.

Christian rose from his seat, then hesitated.

He'd changed his mind. Mariah recognized that look.

"Will Duke mind?" he asked, scanning the room.

"I'm sure he won't, since he's dancing with Angie Hughes."

Mariah had no idea whether Duke was or not, but it sounded good.

A ballad, a slow, melancholy song about tormented lovers, had just begun. Christian drew her into his arms and held her loosely.

"How are your hands?" he asked in a concerned voice.

"Fine. Dotty says the bandages can come off soon." Her head moved closer to his, and soon her crown was tucked under his chin. It seemed so perfect, so natural, to be in his embrace this way.

"Is everything working out for you at the lodge?"

He certainly seemed full of questions. For her part, Mariah would've preferred to close her eyes and give herself over to the music. And the dream.

"Karen and Matt have been wonderful. I—I don't know what I would've done without them. Everyone's been so good to me." It was true—almost everyone had stopped by to see her, to wish her well. While she hadn't made any decisions about rebuilding, she felt the support of her friends, the whole community.

"If you need anything..."

"I don't," and because he couldn't seem to take a hint, Mariah started to hum along with the song.

"That's a lovely song, isn't it?" Christian asked next.

Mariah groaned. "Christian," she whispered. "Please shut up."

He tensed, then chuckled lightly. It was probably the boldest thing she'd ever said to him, but Mariah didn't care. This was *her* fantasy, and she wasn't about to let him ruin it with idle chatter.

If he *did* insist on making small talk, she wanted him to tell her how beautiful she looked. It wasn't Duke she was thinking of when she chose the denim skirt with the white eyelet hem. Nor was it the prospect of an evening with *Duke* that had prompted her to dab on her brand-new—and terribly expensive—French perfume.

Her smile sagged with disappointment. She should've known Christian wouldn't live up to her fantasy. Shaking her head, Mariah smiled softly to herself.

"Something amuses you?"

"You aren't supposed to talk," she reminded him.

He brought back his head just enough to look at her.

"This is my fantasy," she announced without thinking.

"Your fantasy?"

"Never mind."

"No, tell me," he said.

He was going to ruin everything with this incessant talking. "Just shut up and hold me."

His laughter stirred the hair at her temple, but she noticed that his arms tightened fractionally around her.

"What about kissing you?"

"Yes," she whispered eagerly. But because she didn't want to be the focus of any further attention, she added, "not here, though."

"Is that part of the fantasy, too?"

"Yes."

"Do you have someplace special in mind?" he asked. "For me to kiss you, that is."

Anywhere but on the dance floor. She wasn't given an opportunity to say more, however, because they were interrupted by Lanni and Charles.

"Christian. It's about time you showed up. Where've you been all evening?" Charles asked.

"Around," Christian answered shortly.

Mariah noticed how he attempted to steer her away, but they were trapped in a maze of other couples.

"Mariah, that's a lovely color on you," Lanni commented.

"Thanks." She cast a forlorn look at Christian.

"Listen—"

"Stop," Christian said to his brother, and held up one hand. "We don't mean to be rude, but you're interrupting a dream here."

"A dream?" Charles repeated. He apparently thought this was some kind of joke.

"A fantasy," Mariah elaborated. She wasn't sure what possessed her to keep talking but the words seemed to flow without volition. "Christian was about to kiss me, and he can't do that if folks are going to keep interrupting us."

Charles burst out laughing, but stopped abruptly when Lanni glared at him. "Sorry."

"There," Christian whispered to Mariah, "is that better?" He smiled down at her, and the compulsion to stand on tiptoe and thank him with a kiss was a powerful one indeed.

As Lanni and Charles tactfully withdrew, Mariah felt a moment's horror—an intrusion of reality. "I can't believe I said that—about the fantasy."

Christian blinked a couple of times. "I can't believe I said what I did, either." Then he lifted one shoulder in a shrug. "Oh, well . . ." He smiled roguishly.

Mariah smiled back, and awaited his kiss. Then, in plain view of his oldest brother and the entire community, Christian cupped the back of her head and eased his mouth toward Mariah's. His lips met hers with a tenderness that made her go limp in his arms. Soon they gave up the pretense of dancing altogether.

He ended the kiss with a reluctance that said he'd thoroughly enjoyed being part of her fantasy. She knew he wanted to continue—and would have, had they been anyplace else. She opened her eyes slowly and noticed that he was studying her, a baffled look on his face.

The music ended.

Christian dropped his arms and took a step back. "Thank you for the dance," he said when he'd escorted her to her chair.

Duke approached them, looking smug. "I see you're attempting to steal my date." But his tone was humorous, and there was no sign of rancor.

Christian seemed decidedly uncomfortable. "Would it be all right if I talked to Mariah a minute?"

"Are you sure all you're going to do is talk?"

"Yes." Christian sighed.

"Someone might ask me how *I* feel," Mariah suggested in a low voice. She sat down to remove her shoes, but her feet were swollen, and she had to yank the shoes back and forth to pull them off her feet.

By the time she'd finished, Christian had returned with two glasses of punch. He sat down next to her and cleared his throat. "I started out this conversation by thanking you. It would've hurt Midnight Sons badly to lose Duke." He downed the entire contents of his glass in one giant swallow. His gaze seemed fixed on a point at the opposite side of the gym.

"I'm glad I could help."

"Would you be willing to help us again?" he asked, glancing briefly at her.

"How?"

"I offered Duke a twenty percent increase in his wages if he'd stay on. I'd be willing to make the same offer to you if you'd agree to come back and work for Midnight Sons."

Mariah gasped. The request itself didn't shock her, but she took offense at the inducement he'd used. "Is that what the kiss was all about?" she asked, struggling to hold in her anger.

"No." He met her gaze straight on. "I swear the kiss had nothing to do with this." His face fell. "I'm sorry, Mariah," he said, vaulting to his feet. "I really bungled that. You must think I'm a complete jerk. Forget I asked." He started to walk away and she stopped him.

"Christian."

He whirled around, and his eyes were so hopeful she had to restrain herself from laughing.

"I haven't made any long-term plans yet. The fire...well, it raised a number of questions regarding my future." She took a deep breath. "I'll come back to Midnight Sons on two conditions."

"Name them."

"One, Ben has to agree, because technically I still work for him."

"No problem. Ben's a good friend, and he knows Sawyer and I are going crazy without you."

She smiled, agreeing that Ben would willingly let her go. Although he appreciated her help, it was all too apparent she wasn't cut out for waitressing.

"Second," she said, "I'll only agree to work for you—"

"Great!"

"Wait, I haven't finished."

The look on his face was almost comically expectant.

"I'll work for you," she continued, "but only until you can find a permanent replacement."

CHAPTER EIGHT

WHEN CHRISTIAN ENTERED the Midnight Sons office Tuesday morning, he was met by the welcoming scent of a freshly brewed pot of coffee.

"Good morning, Christian," Mariah said cheerfully.

It was all he could do not to close his eyes and exhale a deep, fervent breath of relief. His life was about to return to normal. Mariah was back. The temptation to kiss her—to show her how grateful he was—nearly overwhelmed him.

"Would you care for some coffee?" she asked, automatically pouring him a cup.

"Please." Christian saw that her hands were free from the bulky bandages. Gauze was lightly wrapped around her palms, giving her the use of her fingers.

He sat down at his desk and resisted the urge to lace his hands behind his head and prop his feet up. He figured Mariah might perceive that as overconfidence, and the last thing he wanted to do was annoy her.

"Here you go," she murmured, setting the mug down in front of him.

Christian beamed her a smile of heartfelt appreciation. At his first sip, however, he grimaced. She'd added cream and sugar. Still, his disappointment was minimal; she could've added horseradish and he wouldn't have complained. In time, maybe ten or twenty years, she'd learn he liked his coffee black.

Mariah was back and right now that was all that mattered.

The morning sped past with such ease it was well after noon before Christian noticed the time.

"I'm going over to Ben's for lunch," he told his brother.

"Okay," Sawyer answered distractedly. "Don't forget this is my afternoon off. I'm flying Abbey in for an ultrasound later."

"I didn't forget." Christian smiled to himself. His brother made a great father.

Ben was busy flipping hamburgers on the griddle when Christian entered the café. "You can put on an extra burger for me," he called, and hopped onto a stool.

"You want fries with that?" Ben called back.

Christian shook his head. "Do you have any fresh potato salad?"

"Not today," Ben told him. "How about macaroni?"

"Sure." He was easy to please, especially today.

The bell over the door chimed, and Charles walked in. He sat on the stool next to Christian. "You alone?" he asked.

Christian looked pointedly at the empty stool on his other side. "So it seems. What makes you ask?"

Charles shrugged and pulled out the menu from behind the sugar canister. "I thought you might be taking Mariah to lunch," he said absently as he scanned the selections he'd seen perhaps a thousand times before.

"Why would I do that?" Christian asked, finding the question curious.

"Why not? You're the one who was kissing her in the middle of the school gymnasium. I assumed you two were an item now."

Ben walked past them to a middle-aged couple sitting at a table in the back of the café. "Be right with you, Charles."

"No problem."

"Mariah and I are not an item," Christian explained evenly. The kiss meant nothing. He had half a mind to explain that he happened to be playing along with that little game of hers, but decided against it. His explanation was sure to give his brother extra ammunition.

Charles arched one brow. "If you say so."

"I do," Christian said. It irked him that his own brother, someone whose judgment he trusted, hadn't been able to tell the difference between fantasy and reality, between a "dream" kiss and waking love.

Fortunately Ben delivered his hamburger at that moment. He took Charles's order, then promptly disappeared to the kitchen.

"I talked to Mom this morning," Charles announced.

They didn't often hear from their mother. Christian made an effort to keep in touch with Ellen, had, in fact, visited her only weeks earlier, but she'd remarried and lived a full life in British Columbia now. She loved to travel and took frequent trips with her new husband. Books remained an important part of her life, especially since Robert owned several bookstores. She was independent of her sons now and very much her own woman.

"She said something curious," Charles murmured thoughtfully; he seemed a bit awed, even shaken. "She was telling me how much she enjoyed having Scott and

Susan with her. Then, out of the blue, she said that the three of us were her...connection to life.''

Christian frowned. "Her connection to life?"

"Yes. Now that both Sawyer and I are married and Abbey's pregnant, she said she's begun to feel freer to keep in touch with us. To reach out more often. Apparently she was afraid of intruding in our lives."

"There's no need for her to feel that way."

"That's what I told her, but she dismissed it. She told me she's had to stop herself for years from playing too large a role in our lives. Frankly I don't understand it. I thought she *preferred* to keep her distance. I don't know about you, but I had the feeling the three of us were reminders of all those unhappy years she lived in Hard Luck."

"They weren't all unhappy."

"Perhaps not, but it seemed that way," Charles said. "I assumed that because she has a new life now, she's comfortable with the separation."

"Yes and no." Christian, as the son closest to his mother, spoke with a certain authority.

"I told her that," Charles said, smiling, "and you should've heard the lecture I got. It was pointed out to me that, as her children, we represent her past, share her present and form her future. That's the connection-to-life stuff she was talking about."

"It sounds as though you two cleared the air."

"Yes," Charles agreed, "only I wasn't aware we'd been at odds."

"You weren't," Christian assured him. "All you both needed was a bit of...clarification."

Charles said nothing more for several moments. Then, finally, "She loved him, you know."

"Dad?"

Charles nodded. "For a time I wondered about that, but I realize now how deeply she cared for him. It wasn't a perfect marriage, but they loved each other in their own ways."

"No marriage is perfect," Christian muttered, and bit into his hamburger. He'd leave all that happy-ever-after stuff to Charles and Sawyer. He was thirty-one and had no intention of settling down. Not for a good long while.

"I don't know about no marriage being perfect," Charles said, grinning broadly. "But I'm damn happy with the current state of *mine.*"

"Sure, but you and Lanni are newlyweds."

Charles shook his head in a kind of wonder. "It seems like we've always been together. I'm happy, Chris, happier than I can remember being in many years."

Christian was pleased for his brother, but he reminded himself again that married life wasn't for him.

"Here you are," Ben said, bringing Charles his turkey sandwich. "Now I can take a load off my feet." He pulled up a stool and sat on the opposite side of the counter. "I've been busier than a one-handed piano player," he said with a heavy sigh.

"Do you miss Mariah?" Christian asked, feeling slightly guilty.

"What do you think?" Ben responded. "Of course I miss her. She might have confused orders and broken a few dishes, but she lent a willing hand. And the customers loved her—not to mention her pies. The fact is, I'm going to hire someone else as soon as I can get around to it."

"Good," Charles murmured between bites. "It's about time you did."

"That's what I've been saying." Ben wiped his brow with his forearm. "And I don't intend to put it off, either."

Christian finished his burger and slid the empty plate away. Ben reached for the dish and stuck it in a stack behind the counter. "People have been talking about you and Mariah all morning," he mentioned casually. "You sure have set tongues wagging." Ben chuckled. "What's this I hear about you kissing her in front of half the town?"

Christian ignored the question. "Talking? Who's talking, and what are they saying?"

"Most folks around here seem to think you two're as good as married."

Charles burst out laughing. "That's what you get, little brother. If you don't want people to talk, then I suggest you don't dance with Mariah again. Especially if you're going to take part in her fantasies."

"It's not like that," Christian told Ben, pretending not to hear Charles. "Mariah and I are . . . friends. Good friends. Nothing more."

"Sawyer and I are brothers *and* friends," Charles said lightly, "but you don't see me kissing him."

"Very funny," Christian muttered sarcastically.

He wasn't about to get involved in a verbal battle with Charles and Ben. He'd let them have their fun. They could think what they wanted, but he knew the truth and for that matter, so did Mariah.

Christian slipped off the stool, looked at his tab and slapped the money down on the counter. In his eagerness to make a clean getaway, he nearly collided with Bill Landgrin.

They eyed each other warily. Bill hadn't been at the Labor Day dance, and for that Christian was grateful.

"Hello, Bill," he said. Even if he didn't think much of the other man, there was no need to be rude.

Bill acknowledged the greeting with an inclination of his head. "I hear you've decided to marry Mariah, after all."

"What?" Christian exclaimed. He was becoming frustrated with having to defend himself against this crazy talk. "Who told you that?" he demanded, and sent an accusing glare toward Charles and Ben.

"Not those two, if that's what you're thinking," Bill told him.

"Then who?" Rumors of this kind had to be stopped before they did some damage.

"Just about everyone I've talked to this morning. They all saw you kiss Mariah."

"Just because I kissed her doesn't mean I'm going to marry her! That's insane!"

"Everyone knows how she feels about you."

"Like hell," Christian said, unwilling to listen. After all, she'd accepted Duke's invitation to the dance, which disproved *that* theory.

"Why else do you think the single men in town haven't beaten a path to her door?" Bill asked. "We knew it wouldn't do a damn bit of good, because she'd set her sights on you from the first moment she arrived. Oh, she was nice enough to the rest of us, but we all knew we didn't stand a chance."

"If you believe she's interested in me, then why'd you ask her to the dance?"

"Because she wasn't working for you anymore. I figured she'd given up beating her head against a brick wall, pining for you, but I was wrong. She's as stuck on you as ever. Poor woman."

Christian decided to ignore the last part. "There's nothing between Mariah and me." He was getting tired of having to explain it.

"That's not what I hear."

"And I'm saying whatever you heard isn't true." Christian had to struggle to keep his voice level.

"Then you don't mind if the rest of us pursue her," Bill asked, meeting his gaze evenly.

Christian opened his mouth to object, explain that he felt a responsibility for Mariah's welfare, but snapped it closed. If he did protest, Bill would discount everything he'd just said.

"Sure," he muttered, "but you don't need my permission." He'd talk to Mariah himself, Christian decided, and offer her some advice regarding the so-called eligible men in Hard Luck.

As soon as he could extricate himself from the conversation, Christian made his way back to the office.

Duke had returned from the mail run into Fairbanks and was finishing up his paperwork when Christian stepped into the trailer. Mariah was nowhere in sight, and the pilot sat on a corner of the desk, one foot squarely planted on the floor, the other dangling. "So, how does it feel to have Mariah back?"

Christian laughed. "Like a reprieve from the warden."

Duke set the clipboard aside. "Are you and Mariah going to make a formal announcement soon?"

"A what?" Christian's patience was shot. "Listen, Duke, I wish you and everyone else would get this straight. Mariah and I are *not* romantically involved. We never have been and we never will be."

The pilot didn't bother to conceal his surprise. "You're not?"

"Absolutely not!" To Christian's relief, Mariah came out from the back room just then. "Ask her yourself," he said heatedly, gesturing in her direction.

"Ask me what?" She looked from one man to the other.

"There appears to be a rumor about us floating around town." Christian folded his arms over his chest.

"Well, if you two aren't involved, what were you doing kissing in front of the entire town?" Duke asked.

If Christian had to explain this one more time, he would scream. "It wasn't what it looked like!"

Duke rubbed a hand across his beard with a reflective expression. "It looked obvious enough to me."

"Tell him, Mariah," Christian said.

She stared at him blankly.

"Mariah," he said through gritted teeth, "this isn't funny anymore. *Tell him.*"

"What do you want me to say?"

"The truth! That you and I are not involved. That we're nothing more than friends."

She turned to Duke, and it seemed to take her a long time to speak. "Christian and I are not involved. We're...nothing more than friends."

Christian tossed his hands in the air. "I rest my case."

IT WAS EXTREMELY unfortunate, Mariah felt, that she'd lacked the nerve to empty the coffeepot over Christian's head. The man was an insensitive lout.

They were trapped together in the office all afternoon, and her anger simmered just below the surface, threatening to explode. The first time she slammed a file drawer closed, he leapt up from his chair. He looked at her and, coward that she was, all she did in response was smile. This was her problem in a nutshell. Christian

O'Halloran had abused her good-naturedness from the first.

And she'd let him.

"I don't blame you for being angry," Christian said.

She sat back and studied him carefully. "You don't?"

"Of course not. It makes me angry too. The entire town is talking about us, and it's grossly unfair—to you *and* me."

Mariah clamped her teeth tightly shut as her frustration mounted.

"There must be some way we can dispel these rumors."

"You seem to be doing a fine job of that," she replied sweetly. If he noticed the sarcasm in her voice, he ignored it.

"I've been thinking," Christian said, leaning back in his worn vinyl chair.

"A painful process no doubt," she muttered.

Once again he chose to overlook her derisive comment. "I'm sure you're just as embarrassed by all this gossip as I am." He paused, laughing with what sounded like rather forced heartiness. "Bill Landgrin went so far as to claim you've been in love with me for months. Can you believe that? What a crock."

"Exactly!" She needed her head examined, and the sooner the better.

"He asked did I mind if he asked you out." He eyed her speculatively. "I couldn't very well tell him I did."

"Do you?"

"Well, yes . . ."

"You don't like Bill?"

"I like him fine, but I don't trust him." Christian's eyes grew dark. "I don't think you should, either."

She knew exactly the type of man Bill Landgrin was. Never once had she seriously considered dating him, but she wasn't about to tell Christian that.

"Duke's worth ten Bill Landgrins."

Mariah didn't comment.

"Ralph's a decent sort, too," Christian said, chewing thoughtfully on the end of his pencil.

"Are you suggesting I date Duke or Ralph?" The man had a certain effrontery, she'd say that for him.

"Sure," he answered cheerfully. "Why not?"

"I don't happen to be attracted to either one of them."

Christian threw down the pencil. "You're right, that could present a problem. I'll tell you what," he said, brightening, "I'll take care of this problem myself."

"Good." She didn't know what he had in mind, but it was sure to be amusing.

Mariah liked to think of herself as an even-tempered person, but if she listened to much more of Christian's bizarre advice, she'd turn into a homicidal maniac. Her first victim would be O'Halloran brother number three!

"I'll be back in a minute," he said, purposefully walking out of the office. "I've got to stop off at the house." He was halfway out the door when he turned and flashed her one of his devil-may-care grins. "We haven't got a thing to worry about. I've got a terrific idea."

"I'll just bet," she muttered, but as before her sarcasm was wasted on him.

True to his word, Christian returned five minutes later, slightly breathless. He flashed her another grin and waved a small black telephone directory at her.

"What's that?" It might not have been a good idea to ask, but she couldn't resist.

His eyes twinkled. "Exactly what it looks like. My little black book."

True to her prediction, this was going to be amusing. Crossing her arms, Mariah sat down and waited. "What do you plan to do with it?"

"Get a date, what else? There are a number of women in Fairbanks who'll remember me."

"A date?"

"Yeah," he murmured, leafing through the pages. "Since you aren't keen on dating Duke or Ralph—"

"They aren't the only eligible men in town."

"That's right," he said, reaching for the telephone receiver and pinning it between his shoulder and ear. "But there's more than one way to skin a cat," he said, and winked at her. "Or in this case, kill a rumor."

Mariah rolled her eyes dramatically.

"Hello, Ruthie?" Christian propped his feet on the corner of his desk and wore a cocky grin. "It's Christian."

Mariah watched as the grin slowly faded.

"Christian O'Halloran from Hard Luck. Remember?"

The smile was back in place.

"Yeah, that's me. Right. How are you? Wonderful. Wonderful."

A shocked expression came into his eyes. "Married! When did that happen?"

He looked at Mariah and shrugged, free hand palm up in a gesture that said this had come as a complete surprise.

"Congratulations. Yes, of course. You should have sent me an invitation... Oh, you did. Sorry, we've been real busy around here the past few months... Oh, it's been a year now? That long? Well, listen, I won't keep you... Pregnant? Oh...wow. Great. Keep in touch, okay?"

Mariah had to turn her back to him to keep from laughing out loud.

"Scratch Ruthie," he said. "But don't despair. I've got plenty of other names."

"I'm sure you do." The phone rang and Mariah answered it. While she was dealing with the call, she watched Christian reach for his phone a second time. Because her attention was distracted, she couldn't follow what was happening, but from the expression he wore, it seemed to be a similar experience.

Mariah took down her caller's information and replaced the telephone receiver.

"Carol's involved with someone else, too." He flipped through the pages, muttering under his breath, dismissing one name after another. Tanya? No, he'd heard she'd gone to California. Hmm, what about Tiffany? No, they'd had that big fight. Sandra? Never really liked her. A number of times he paused and tapped his finger against his teeth as he contemplated a name. Gail? He tried the number; it was disconnected.

"It seems I've been out of circulation," he said to no one in particular. "Ruthie married. Damn, we used to have a lot of fun together. Where did the time go?" He picked up the phone and tried again.

Mariah didn't want to listen, but she couldn't make herself stop.

"Pam," he said in a carefree voice. "It's Christian O'Halloran from Hard Luck. It's been two years?" He sounded shocked. "That long? Really? How've you been?"

Five solid minutes passed, during which Christian didn't speak. He opened his mouth a couple of times, but couldn't seem to get a word in edgewise.

"I'm sorry to hear that," he finally said in a rush. "Married—only lasted three months. Divorce final this week..." He closed his eyes and waited, tapping one finger on his desk. "Pam—listen, I'm at work. I don't have a lot of time...I'll call you again soon. So sorry to hear about your troubles." He replaced the receiver as if he couldn't do it fast enough.

Slowly he raised his eyes to Mariah. "Pam's been married *and* divorced since the last time I saw her."

"This doesn't sound like it's going so well." It was too much to ask to keep the glee out of her voice. If he was having a difficult time finding a date, then that was fine with her.

"Vickie," he said, suddenly triumphant. "She used to be crazy about me."

"Really?" More fool she.

"I'm sure she'll be available."

It didn't escape Mariah's notice that the woman who was supposedly enamored of him wasn't his first choice. Now, why didn't that surprise her?

Christian punched out the telephone number, but Mariah saw that most of his cockiness had disappeared. Apparently Vickie was unavailable, because he spoke a few, brief sentences in a near-monotone.

"I reached her answering machine," he said. He looked mildly discouraged. "I wonder if Vickie's married," he said, and the thought appeared to sadden him.

But she wasn't; an hour later, Vickie, the smitten one, returned his call.

Christian perked up like a freshly watered flower. "*Hello,* Vickie. So how's it going?"

As best she could, Mariah tuned him out. This time, she didn't care to listen. Vickie, Mariah feared, would sound all too familiar. It would be like listening to herself.

"Saturday night?" Christian sounded pleased. "Dinner. A movie? Sure, anything you want to see. Great. I'll look forward to it." A short pause. "I'll be in Fairbanks around six. See you then."

When he finished, Mariah glanced toward his desk. Christian sat with his fingers linked behind his head, elbows jutting out. He wore a wide, satisfied grin.

"Our troubles are over," he said, and paused as if she should thank him for the noble sacrifice he was making on her behalf.

"Wonderful," she said.

"Don't you see?" Christian asked impatiently. "Once everyone in Hard Luck finds out I'm dating another woman, the gossip will stop."

"Really?" The man had mush for brains. "And how will people learn that, since you're flying into Fairbanks to see Vickie? Or was that Pam? No, Carol." She was being deliberately obtuse.

His smile was stiff. "Vickie. And people will know, because I intend to tell them."

"Perfect," she said without enthusiasm.

"You don't sound happy."

"You're wrong. I'm delighted." She checked her watch and realized it was quitting time. In more ways than one. Reaching for her sweater, she cast him a deceptively calm smile. "See you in the morning."

Then she walked out the door, suppressing the urge to slam it.

VICKIE. CHRISTIAN COULDN'T believe he hadn't thought of her sooner. He'd always gotten along famously with her. He wondered if she still worked at the bank.

Not until he'd started making the calls did he realize he'd been out of touch for so long.

Tucking the small phone directory into his shirt pocket, he frowned. Mariah couldn't seem to leave the office fast enough. And she didn't seem to appreciate that he was putting his ego on the line, calling his former girlfriends after so long an absence.

More than a year.

Not that he'd ever been a Romeo. Like the rest of the men in Hard Luck, he flew into Fairbanks—or he used to—for some R and R whenever the mood struck him.

But a *year*.

Then it hit him. Hard Luck had started bringing in women right around that time. That explained it.

Turning off his computer and the office lights, Christian left for the evening.

As he was walking home, his eight-year-old niece rode past him on a bike. She hit the brakes, skidding on the dirt.

"Did you hear?" she called back to him excitedly.

"Hear what?" Christian asked.

"Mom and Sawyer—I mean Dad—just got back from the doctor's appointment in Fairbanks."

Christian vaguely remembered Sawyer's saying something about flying into Fairbanks that afternoon because Abbey was having an ultrasound. Funny they'd missed each other at the office. Not that Sawyer was obligated to check in with him of course.

"Mom's having a baby girl."

"A girl," Christian repeated, smiling. Ellen would be pleased.

"They got pictures of the baby and everything. I was on my way over to tell Chrissie. Bethany's going to have a baby, too."

"They have a picture of the baby?" This was something Christian wanted to see. A picture of an unborn baby.

"Well," Susan said, chewing on her lower lip, "they said it was a picture, but all it looked like to me was a bunch of black blurry lines."

"A little girl," Christian repeated.

"That's what the doctor said."

"That's great."

"Dad thinks so," Susan said, and laughed, "but I think he would've been happy with a boy, too."

"My brother's easy to please."

Susan tried to climb back on the bicycle, but was having some difficulty. Christian walked over to give her a hand by holding the bike steady. She clambered up and grinned at him. "Thanks, Uncle Christian."

"You're welcome."

Susan took off at breakneck speed, leaning over the handlebars in her eagerness to reach her friend's house with the news. So, Mitch and Bethany were going to add to their family, too. Hard Luck was about to experience a population explosion.

Christian hadn't gone more than half a block when Scott came racing down the road. "Did you see Susan?" he asked, his face red with anger.

"What if I did?"

"She stole my bike."

"She wanted to tell her friend your mom's having a girl."

"Well, the doctor might be wrong," Scott grumbled and kicked at the dirt with the toe of his tennis shoe.

"I take it you were hoping for a boy?"

Scott shrugged. "We got enough girls in the family already. I asked Mom if she'd be willing to have another baby, to make sure the next one's a boy—and you know what she said?"

Christian shook his head.

"She said not to count on that, but if she doesn't have a boy, then either Lanni would when her and Charles have babies. Or maybe Mariah after you marry her."

CHAPTER NINE

CHRISTIAN WAS HAVING a pleasant evening, but he sensed his date wasn't. Vickie was resolutely silent as they sat across from each other in the all-night diner. They'd been to dinner and a movie, and Christian's spirits were high.

"Did I mention the time Mariah made the filing cabinet fall over?" He could laugh about the incident now, but he hadn't found it funny at the time. She'd been trying to shift the cabinet herself, just to spite him. Then when he'd hurried over to help, she'd tripped—and the cabinet had tumbled and fallen on his foot. He'd limped for a week.

To this day the top drawer didn't close properly. Leave it to Mariah.

He relayed the story, laughing as he told it; Vickie, however, hadn't so much as cracked a smile.

Confused, Christian lowered his coffee mug to the table, and his laughter faded.

"Do you realize," Vickie asked, her gaze direct and not the least bit amused, "that you've spent the entire evening talking about another woman?"

He had? No way. "Who?" he asked. Surely Vickie was exaggerating. That couldn't possibly be true. Okay, so he'd mentioned Mariah and the filing cabinet, but the only reason he'd told Vickie about that incident was because it was so funny.

"First, I heard about the fire that destroyed Mariah's cabin, followed by—"

"I was updating you on the news in Hard Luck," he broke in, defending himself. "Didn't I also mention that Sawyer's married and Abbey's expecting? And I told you about Charles and Lanni, didn't I?"

"Sure, in passing," Vickie said, flipping a strand of hair over her shoulder. Christian had always liked her long, golden hair. Straight and silky, it reached halfway down her back.

"Then there was the story about Mariah's luggage flying open on the runway—"

"You're making more of this than necessary." Christian didn't remember Vickie as the jealous type, but then, he didn't really know her that well.

"I don't hear from you in over a year, and now all of a sudden you can't wait to take me out. I have to tell you, Christian, your suggestion that we get together is becoming suspicious to me."

"Suspicious?"

"Like you're proving something to yourself and using me to do it."

"Not true," he replied in annoyance. "There's a perfectly logical reason I haven't been in touch. You heard we, uh, invited some women to town, didn't you?"

"Of course I heard about it! Midnight Sons had the whole state talking." She pinched her lips together in a show of disapproval and folded her arms. "Bringing in women! It's the most ridiculous thing I've ever heard. What's wrong with the women right here in Fairbanks?"

Christian wasn't wading into that muddy pond, so he ignored the question. "Well, it explains why you didn't hear from me," he muttered.

"I'd have moved to Hard Luck if you'd given me a reason to." Her look was full of meaning, and her gaze firmly held his.

Christian swallowed tightly. "Sure," he said, feeling more than a little uncomfortable with the way the conversation had turned. "There're plenty of single men left in Hard Luck. You'd be welcome to move to town any time."

She glared at him. "I'm not asking about other men," she snapped. "I want to know about *you*."

"Me?" Someone must have apparently raised the temperature in the restaurant, because the room suddenly felt suffocatingly hot. Christian resisted the urge to ease his finger along the inside of his collar.

"Well, I'm certainly not interested in the guy who runs that café."

"Ben." Christian leapt on his friend's name. "Why, he's great."

"Get real, O'Halloran." The hair he'd recently admired flew back over her shoulder like a blast of gold. The glare returned full force. "What I want to know is why it was so all-fired important to call me now, especially with all those women you've managed to bring to Hard Luck." The challenge was impossible to ignore.

Christian decided it would be poor timing indeed to explain that he was hoping to kill the rumors that romantically linked him with Mariah.

"I've been awfully busy lately... and, well, I decided it was time to renew old acquaintances."

"It wouldn't be so bad if I hadn't been so damn eager to see you," she said, and slapped her purse on the table. "You call good ol' Vickie, and then spend the entire evening talking about another woman."

"I don't know what you mean."

She threw him a disgusted look, then slid out of the booth.

"What are you doing?" Christian was stunned; she was actually leaving.

Vickie offered him a bright smile. "I'm going home."

"I'll drive you." She appeared to find his company objectionable, but to leave the diner without him added insult to injury.

"No, thanks," she said stiffly.

Christian hurriedly paid for the coffee and followed Vickie out of the diner. "What did I do that was so terrible?" It was embarrassing, but he suspected he was actually whining. He'd never experienced this kind of trouble with a woman before.

Damn it, Vickie had changed in the past year; then again, maybe she wasn't the only one. Christian had the distinct feeling he'd done some changing of his own.

"What did you do?" Vickie repeated, standing outside the coffee shop. She sighed loudly. "Listen, you're a great guy, but whatever there was between us is over—and was a long time ago. I guess I needed this date to prove to myself how over you I am. It's also pretty clear that you're crazy about Mariah."

Out of habit, Christian opened his mouth to deny everything, but Vickie didn't give him the opportunity.

"I don't know what you were trying to prove, but I resent being used."

"There's no need to get on your high horse. If you don't want to go out with me again, fine. But at least let me drive you home." It was a matter of pride, if nothing else.

Vickie agreed, and they rode silently back to her apartment complex. When he parked, she turned to face him. "I hope you manage to set everything straight with Mariah."

Christian didn't bother to correct her. He wasn't "crazy about" Mariah or involved with her or anything else, but he'd be wasting his breath to tell Vickie that.

"Promise me one thing," she said.

"Sure."

"Send me a wedding invitation. I'd like to meet the woman who tagged you."

This time Christian couldn't stop himself. "I'm not marrying Mariah!"

He wanted to shout it again. He *wasn't* marrying her—was he? Sure, he found her attractive and damn it all, he'd kissed her and wouldn't mind doing it again. But that didn't mean marriage. It shouldn't. True, he felt protective of her, but that was because...because he felt responsible. Wasn't it? The hell if he knew.

Vickie laughed softly and patted his cheek. "You protest far too much for me to believe you. Just remember what I said. I want an invitation to the wedding."

FIRST THING Monday morning, Mariah took out the file of applications Christian had collected the previous year. She was reading through the stack of them when he arrived.

"Morning," he said curtly, refusing to meet her eyes.

"Morning," she returned, her mood matching his.

The coffee was brewed and ready, but she didn't pour him a mug. He could darn well get his own, she decided. Either he was unwilling to do that or not interested, because he sat down at his desk and immediately turned on his computer.

"How'd your big date go?" she couldn't resist asking. This penchant for emotional pain was probably something she should investigate. Besides, even if he'd had a perfectly miserable evening, he'd never let her know.

"Fine," he growled. "Has Ralph been in yet?"

"No," she answered.

Christian glanced at her and appeared surprised by her terse reply. "Is something bothering you?" he asked.

"Not a thing," she assured him ever so sweetly. She refused to give him cause for complaint, and every time he glanced her way she made sure she was the picture of contentment. Not that he looked over very often.

Whatever was on the computer screen commanded his full attention. He sat up straight in his chair and peered at it for long minutes. Finally, without lifting his eyes, he asked abruptly, "Where's Ted?"

"Don't know."

"I'm going over to the bunkhouse to see if I can find him."

"I thought you asked about Ralph."

"Nope, I need to see Ted." He left as if it was a dire emergency.

He didn't close down his computer, and out of curiosity, Mariah got up to look at his screen. He'd been reviewing the flight schedule for the week. The mail runs into Fairbanks were made on a rotation basis. Ralph had made the run the previous week, but Ted was scheduled to do it this week.

Ted appeared in the office soon afterward wearing a forlorn expression. "Christian asked me to tell you he'll be the one going into Fairbanks this morning."

Mariah made a note of the change. "Thanks, Ted."

So Christian was interested in flying into Fairbanks. That could mean only one thing.

He would be seeing Vickie again.

KAREN CALDWELL HUMMED softly to herself as she placed the Noah's-ark stencil along the bottom of the freshly painted wall. The baby's nursery was coming along nicely. She felt a constant undercurrent of excitement these days. Preparing the room, buying clothes, reading infant-care books—it all made the baby seem so *real*.

"Karen." Matt's voice boomed from the lobby.

"In here," she shouted over her shoulder. Unfolding her legs, she got to her feet, eager to talk to her husband. All at once, the room started to spin and she promptly sat back down again.

Matt must've seen what happened because he rushed in. "Honey, what's wrong?"

She smiled up at his worried face, loving him all the more for his concern. "Nothing. I'm fine. I guess I just stood up too quickly."

"Getting dizzy like that—are you *sure* you're okay?" he asked. "What about the baby?"

"It happens to everyone now and then, not just pregnant women."

"You're sure?" he asked again. He didn't sound like he believed her.

"Positive."

He still didn't look reassured. "I'd feel better if Dotty checked you out."

"All right," she agreed, "but after lunch." Her appetite had increased lately, and Karen suspected her body was making up for the weight she'd lost the first months of her pregnancy when she'd been so terribly ill.

"Actually," she told him as he led the way into the kitchen, "I feel wonderful." Working on the nursery made the baby's birth seem so close. The crib and other furniture had arrived a few days earlier, and they'd assembled everything over the weekend.

"You look wonderful," her husband told her. He gazed at her intently, then the worried expression fled his eyes and they softened with love.

Karen went about making toasted cheese sandwiches while Matt opened a can of soup. "I have a feeling we're going to lose Mariah soon," Matt said as if the subject had been weighing on his mind.

Karen had been thinking the same thing. "I blame Christian for that. I swear that man left his brains behind somewhere."

"He's a stubborn one, that's for sure."

"You should know," Karen teased.

Matt made a show of protesting. He moved behind her and wrapped his arms around her middle, splaying his hands across her abdomen. "How come Abbey and Sawyer get an ultrasound and we don't?"

"Because I'm under thirty-five, so the doctor didn't think it was necessary. Besides, I'd rather be surprised by the baby's sex."

"Sawyer passed around the picture of the ultrasound over at Ben's this morning, proud as could be over a few blurry lines." Matt sounded a little wistful.

"Do you want a picture to pass around, too?" she asked sympathetically.

He nuzzled her neck. "I guess I do."

"I can ask the doctor at my next appointment. But, Matt, I'd really prefer not to know if we're having a boy or a girl until the baby's born. Agreed?"

"Agreed." He spread kisses down the side of her neck.

Karen yawned unexpectedly. Every afternoon, like clockwork, she slept a good hour, sometimes two. Again she suspected this was her body's way of regaining strength after the first turbulent months of her pregnancy.

"I wish there was something I could do for Mariah," Karen said as she carried the sandwiches to the table.

Matt emptied the soup into two bowls. "I don't know what. She has to make her own decisions, the same way Christian does."

"Maybe you could talk to Christian."

His gaze shot to his wife. "Not a chance. He's got two brothers, but I imagine they feel the same way about all this as we do. If it's anyone's business to say something to Christian, it's theirs. I tried to help Lanni's romance with Charles along and—"

"You did? When?"

"Last year about this time. It didn't work, and I got myself into hot water with my sister. No one appreciates unsolicited advice."

"So what can we do?" Karen asked. She really felt for Mariah.

"Nothing."

"But—"

"I know, sweetheart, but it's not our affair, and neither Christian nor Mariah would take kindly to our interference. They'd resent it."

Sadly Karen acknowledged that he was right.

CHRISTIAN KNEW Mariah was upset about something the minute he returned from the flight into Fairbanks. If ever there was a time he needed to think straight, it had been this morning. That was the reason he'd taken the mail run from Ted.

Mariah had snapped at him earlier, and now she glared at him like a mother bear protecting her cubs—or, maybe, hoping to feed them. One glance told him the only way he was going to walk away whole would be to run for cover.

"I'm back," he said unnecessarily.

She responded by looking daggers at him.

He tried again, ignoring her bad mood. "Where's Sawyer?" His older brother was more accustomed to dealing with women, irrational creatures that they were; he could use Sawyer's help here. He sighed. First Vickie and now Mariah. And to think, *he'd* been the one to suggest bringing women to town.

"Sawyer's out," was the only response she gave him.

"Did he happen to mention where he was going?" he asked tentatively.

"Yes."

Mariah seemed to forget he was her employer. Just because he'd practically kissed her feet when she'd agreed to come back didn't mean she could get uppity with him.

"Do you have any objection to telling me where my brother is?" he asked, hardening his voice.

"None. He said he was going home for lunch."

Sawyer had been doing that more often lately. If he'd been aware of the time, Christian could probably have figured it out for himself.

"Thank you," he said coolly. He sat down at his desk and discovered a number of employment applications spread out across the surface. The very ones he'd read through a dozen times the week before. The very ones he'd rejected.

"What are these out for?" he asked in a way that would inform her his patience wasn't limitless.

"It didn't seem you were in any hurry to hire my replacement," she said without emotion, "so I took the liberty of contacting a few of the applicants myself."

He opened his mouth to object and realized he couldn't. She was right; he wasn't in any hurry to replace her. He told himself it was because he couldn't handle the idea of training a new secretary; it seemed beyond him. Perhaps he was being unfair to Mariah, but he'd hoped that in time she'd agree to come back permanently. Then everything would go back to the way it used to be.

"I take it you found a number of suitable applicants," he said gesturing at his desk.

"I called the ones on your desk. Libby Bozeman has accepted the position. She'll arrive in Hard Luck a week Friday. I printed up the contract and faxed it to her."

"You *hired* her?"

Mariah's back stiffened. "Yes. As I mentioned earlier, you didn't seem to be in a hurry to replace me, so I took matters into my own hands."

"Does Sawyer know?"

"Yes, and he approved Libby."

"I see." Christian knew when he was beaten. He leafed through the papers until he found Libby's application. As he read over the simple form, it amazed him how naive they'd been going into this project. He'd requested only the most basic information. He hadn't even asked for references.

"She looks suitable." For the life of him, Christian couldn't remember interviewing her.

"I talked to a number of the other applicants this morning," Mariah told him in that prim voice of hers. He could always tell when she was put out, because her voice dipped several degrees below freezing.

"Mrs. Bozeman seemed the most qualified."

"She's married?"

"No, but was—until recently."

"Was she married last year when I interviewed her?" he couldn't keep from asking.

"Apparently so."

"I see." He did remember her now, and if his memory served him correctly, she was very qualified. Libby Bozeman was a tall, attractive woman, perhaps in her forties; she knew her mind and had no problem speaking it. A no-nonsense woman. Mariah had chosen well.

"If you have no objection, I'll have an airline ticket sent to her."

"None whatsoever," Christian returned in the same crisp tones.

Neither spoke for several moments. Then, because he had to know, Christian asked. "What about you? Where will you go?" He wondered how Ben felt about taking her back. The café owner was fond of Mariah—for that matter, so was Christian—but it hadn't worked before and he doubted Mariah would be willing to try again.

"Where will I go?" Mariah repeated softly as if considering the question for the first time.

Christian stopped himself from making a number of suggestions, all of which would keep her in Hard Luck.

She looked up at him, and it seemed her eyes were brighter than normal. Slowly she released her breath, and when she spoke her voice faltered slightly. "Somewhere I won't ever have to see you again, Christian O'Halloran."

CHRISTIAN WALKED BACK to his house later that afternoon, his hands buried in his jacket pockets. His spirits dragged along the road like an untied shoelace, threatening to trip him.

Mariah, leaving. Again. Only this time she was leaving more than Midnight Sons. She was leaving Hard Luck. Leaving Alaska. *Leaving him.*

Libby Bozeman. Now that he remembered her, he was sure she'd work out fine, but damn it all, he wanted Mariah. At least this time she'd agreed to stay until Libby could be properly trained.

Even Sawyer seemed to think it was best to let Mariah go. Christian had approached his brother the minute the two were alone, and Sawyer had shrugged and reminded him that they couldn't force her to stay.

When he reached his house, Christian noticed that Scott and Ronny Gold were playing catch with Eagle Catcher in the front yard of Sawyer's home, across the street. Depressed, he sank onto the top porch step, watching the boys' carefree play. Scott and Ronny tossed the stick and Eagle Catcher raced across the yard to retrieve it.

Christian didn't know how long he sat there taking in the scene. Soon it would be dinnertime, but he hadn't the energy to cook, nor did he feel like joining Ben at the café. The fact was, he didn't seem all that hungry.

Susan stuck her head out the door of their house and shouted something Christian couldn't hear. Ronny Gold took off running, but Scott stayed behind with his dog.

Christian envied Sawyer. It had all been so easy for him. Abbey arrived with the kids, and within a month they'd decided to marry. No muss. No fuss. Easy as pie.

"Hiya, Uncle Christian."

Caught up in his misery, Christian hadn't noticed Scott's approach. Now the ten-year-old was standing on the other side of the fence.

"Hello, Scott."

"What's the matter? You don't look so good."

Christian couldn't think of a way to explain his complicated, confused emotions to a child. Hell, he couldn't explain them to himself.

Scott let himself into the yard and sat down on the step below Christian. "Does this have anything to do with Mariah leaving?"

Christian's eyes widened before he realized Scott must've heard Sawyer mentioning the new secretary to Abbey. "Yeah, I guess you could say that."

"You want me to give you some advice on romance? I'm good at that."

"You?"

"Sure. I helped Sawyer before he asked my mom to marry him. I told him about those bath-oil beads that melt in the water."

Christian gently patted the boy's shoulder. It wouldn't be that simple with Mariah. Bath-oil beads weren't going to help *this* situation.

"Matt Caldwell asked me for advice on how to get Karen back, too."

"Matt did?" That surprised Christian. He'd always assumed Matt's reconciliation with his pregnant wife had been quick and effortless. She hadn't been back in Hard Luck long before they'd remarried. Every time he saw them lately, they behaved like newlyweds. It was hard to believe they'd ever been divorced.

"Matt even bought my ice-cream bar for me," Scott told him proudly. "My advice must've worked, 'cause he and Karen got married right after that."

"Good for you."

Scott leaned his back against the step. "You need any advice, I'll help you, too."

"I appreciate the offer, but what's going on between me and Mariah is different."

Scott cocked his head at an angle to look up at Christian. "How's that?"

"I really like Mariah."

"But you aren't sure you love her," Scott finished for him.

"Yes," Christian said, straightening. Scott's insight surprised him.

"I know what you mean," the boy said, sounding mature beyond his years. "It's like me and Chrissie Harris."

It took Christian a moment to remember that Chrissie was Mitch Harris's daughter. Mitch and Bethany had married that summer. "What about you and Chrissie?" he asked.

"Well," Scott said, propping his elbows on the step above. His look was thoughtful. "She's my little sister's best friend and she can be a real pest."

Clearly the boy knew women.

"But I like her," Scott continued with a heartfelt sigh.

Christian couldn't believe how adequately Scott had described his feelings toward Mariah. The woman had driven him to distraction for months now.

"But you know, sometimes I look at Chrissie and think she's got the prettiest eyes of any girl I've ever seen."

Christian was fond of Mariah's eyes, too. The way they drifted closed at the precise moment he knew he needed to kiss her. How prettily her long eyelashes brushed against the high arch of her cheek. How expressive they were, betraying every mood from anger to ecstasy. Her eyes. Oh, yes, she had beautiful eyes.

"Sometimes I think Chrissie's probably the most beautiful girl in the world. Even with freckles."

That, too, accurately described Christian's feelings. He recalled the time he flew to Seattle and had dinner with Allison Reynolds. Outwardly she was a knockout, but he'd found her frivolous and superficial. Mariah, though . . . there wasn't a phony bone in her beautiful body. "Mariah doesn't have freckles, but I know what you mean."

Scott grinned. "I thought you would." Then his expression turned serious. "I like Chrissie because she's a good friend to Susan. I don't know if Susan would've liked living in Hard Luck so much if it wasn't for Chrissie."

Christian mentally reviewed the women who'd come and gone in the past year. A number had stayed and settled in the community, and a number had left. Despite the hardships, despite the cold, Mariah had stayed. He'd misjudged her from the first, believing she'd be one of the first to pack her bags and go.

Scott's deep sigh was expressive. "I think one day I'll probably marry Chrissie Harris."

Christian winced at the word "marry"—it had always made him uncomfortable. "Don't you think you're a bit young to be talking about that sort of thing?"

"Sure, I've got a lot of years yet, and Mom and Dad are already talking about me going to college."

Christian patted the boy's shoulder again, more vigorously this time, proud to call him nephew.

"But I've already decided if I don't marry Chrissie, I want a girl like her."

"Scott!" Susan stood out on the front porch across the street and hollered at the top of her lungs. "Dinner!"

"You'd better run along."

"Yeah. Mom's serving my favorite meat loaf tonight. She got the recipe out of the newspaper a long time ago from some lady who writes an advice column, and it's real good."

"You'd best not keep her waiting then." Christian might not know much about dealing with women, but he knew better than to let his dinner get cold.

"Did I help you any?" Scott asked.

"You did." It was true. "You should think about writing an advice column of your own."

Scott nodded thoughtfully. "I just might, you know. Some day Aunt Lanni wants to start a newspaper in Hard Luck. She might let me do it, too, 'cause we're related."

"If you want, I'll put in a good word for you."

Scott beamed. "Great!"

Advice to the lovelorn from Scott O'Halloran, Hard Luck's hometown expert.

Smiling for the first time since Mariah had announced she was leaving, Christian stood up. His hand was on the front doorknob when something Scott had said struck him.

Scott wanted to marry a girl like Chrissie.

A woman like Mariah. That was what Christian wanted in his life. A woman like Mariah.

MARIAH HADN'T DECIDED what she'd do or where she'd live once Libby Bozeman had been trained. The thought of leaving Hard Luck made her infinitely sad. But she had no choice if she wanted to avoid Christian O'Halloran.

Just thinking about that stubborn, obtuse man made her angry all over again. Angry enough to find it impossible to sit still. Following dinner, she decided to take a walk.

The sun was getting ready to set, and it wouldn't be long before dark settled in, but she didn't let that deter her.

"I'll be back soon," she told Matt and Karen who sat in the swing on the front porch. Karen's head rested against her husband's shoulder, and Matt had one arm about his wife. Much as Mariah loved them both and delighted in their happiness right now it was painful to watch.

Buttoning her sweater, collar pulled up around her ears, she walked briskly for about ten minutes until she was winded.

Night descended faster than she'd anticipated, and not wanting to stumble about in the dark, she started to take a shortcut around the back of the Hard Luck Café.

Apparently Ben had just stepped outside, because the light from the open kitchen door spilled out, lighting her path.

Mariah kept her head down, anxious to be on her way and avoid exchanging pleasantries.

She heard a muffled sound and paused to glance back. At first she saw nothing, then made out a shadowy form. It appeared to be a large animal on the ground, next to the garbage cans Ben kept outside his back door. She hesitated, uncertain if she should venture closer. Lanni had once encountered a bear on the tundra, and just hearing the tale had given Mariah goose bumps.

She took a step, then two, before deciding it was ridiculous to run from her fears. If it was a bear in the shadows, he'd get far more interesting fare from Ben's kitchen than her.

As she approached the light, Mariah realized it wasn't an animal down there in the shadows, but a person.

"Ben?" she whispered. "Ben!"

But Ben didn't stir.

CHAPTER TEN

"BEN." MARIAH FELL to her knees and pressed her finger against the artery in his neck. Again and again she tried to locate a pulse but found none. Her own accelerated at an alarming pace as she realized Ben Hamilton had probably suffered a heart attack.

She left him only long enough to race into the kitchen and call for help. She dialed Mitch's number. Hard as she tried to remain calm, her words were rushed and she felt close to panic.

Forcing herself to breathe deeply and think clearly, she returned to Ben's side and carefully rolled him onto his back. His head lolled to one side and his coloring was poor. She slid her hand behind his neck, then lifted his head and begin to administer CPR. Luckily she'd taken a course in cardiopulmonary resuscitation in college several years back and knew what needed to be done.

"Ben, oh, Ben," she said as she pressed the heel of her hand on his chest and pumped. He wasn't breathing on his own. His heart began again—erratically, but it was beating. She then stopped to administer mouth-to-mouth.

She wasn't sure how long she worked, alternating between the breathing and pumping his heart. It seemed as though an eternity had passed before she heard the sound of footsteps behind her.

"What happened?" Mitch shouted.

"Heart attack," she panted. The two words required an inordinate amount of energy.

Mitch squatted down beside Ben and assisted her, taking over the breathing while she continued to work the older man's heart.

Two emergency medical volunteers arrived at the scene and took over. A crowd started to gather, everyone whispering as Ben was loaded into the back of the ambulance and rushed to the health clinic.

"Mitch!" Bethany cried from behind him. "What's happening?"

Mariah watched Mitch gather his wife into his arms. "It's Ben," he whispered. Bethany's eyes immediately filled with tears.

"His heart?" Her voice trembled and she bit her lower lip. "I knew something wasn't right. He promised me he'd ease up and stop working so hard. He *promised*."

Mitch smoothed the hair away from Bethany's face in a gentle gesture of love and comfort.

"I just found him," Bethany sobbed in agony. "I can't lose him now."

"Are you all right, Mariah?" Sawyer O'Halloran arrived breathless, Abbey following. "We were at Mitch's when you called."

Mariah felt as if she was in a daze, but she managed to nod.

"Are you sure?"

"I'm fine." But she'd never felt this shaky. All at once her bones seemed to dissolve, and she slumped against the side of the building.

"I think you need to sit down," Abbey said, taking Mariah by the hand and leading her into the café. She steered Mariah to a chair, then quickly brewed a pot of tea.

"What's going to happen to Ben?" Mariah asked, praying her meager efforts had been enough to save him. She worried about whether she'd followed the procedure correctly. The CPR class had been years ago, and she might have forgotten something.

"Medical transport is on the way. A medical team will arrive by helicopter in just a little while," Sawyer explained. "Christian's on the radio with them now."

Abbey added a liberal amount of sugar to Mariah's tea and briskly stirred it. "Here," she said, her voice gentle, "drink this."

"How'd you happen to find him?" Sawyer wanted to know.

Mariah explained that she'd gone out for a walk after dinner and been taking a shortcut back to the lodge because of the dark when she found Ben. She trembled as she spoke, remembering how she almost hadn't stopped to check. How she'd nearly given in to the fear of encountering a bear.

"Without you, Ben would've died."

Cupping the mug with both hands, Mariah drank deeply. It went without saying that Ben could still die.

By the time the distinctive sound of the helicopter could be heard in the distance, half the town had gathered by the airfield. Not that there was anything to see or do. People came to lend emotional support to one another, to show Ben that they cared and that he was an important part of their lives. To show him that Hard Luck wouldn't be the same without him. Even though Ben was unconscious, Mariah believed that all this love must touch him in some way.

As the emergency medical technicians wheeled Ben to the plane, the prayers and hopes of the community went with him.

"Any family?" a man called from inside the transport.

Bethany whispered something to Mitch, then hugged him and Chrissie and rushed to climb into the helicopter.

After the helicopter lifted off the runway, everyone started to talk at once. A number of the curious crowded around Mariah, and she repeated the story of how she'd found Ben. People were gathered around Mitch, too, asking questions about Bethany's relationship with Ben. Mariah couldn't hear what he said and was too exhausted to wonder about it right now.

Karen and Matt walked back to the lodge with her. As she headed up the porch steps, Mariah saw Christian. He stood nearby, talking to Sawyer and Charles. His gaze left his brothers and drifted to her. Their eyes met and held for a long moment, before she found the strength to break the contact. Her heart filled with a deep sadness as she turned and entered the lodge.

THE FOLLOWING MORNING Christian was the first to arrive at the Midnight Sons office. He'd spent the better part of the night tossing and turning, unable to sleep. Twice he'd called the hospital and talked to Bethany, and the news was good. Ben had stabilized, and the hospital had scheduled a number of tests. If all went as the doctors expected, Ben would be headed for open-heart surgery early that afternoon.

Worrying about Ben's condition wasn't all that had kept Christian awake. He'd given some thought to what he'd learned last night about his friend—that he was Bethany's natural father. Not surprisingly, it was all over town. People were shocked but more than that, they were genuinely pleased. Christian had also been thinking about Mariah.

He mulled over everything that had happened in the past fourteen months, everything he knew about her, from her courage in coming here to her skill and bravery last night. He considered her compassion, too, her honesty, her sense of humor. He'd misjudged her for so long. *A woman like Mariah.* The words wouldn't stop circling his mind.

If he did marry, and eventually he intended to, he wanted to marry a woman like Mariah. Not a fancy city girl like Allison. Or even one like Vickie, nice though she was. He wanted a woman like Mariah. But if he'd already found her, then—

The door to the office opened, cutting him off in midthought. Mariah walked in, and she looked as tired as Christian felt.

"The coffee's almost ready," he told her. He stood in front of the machine and waited for the liquid to finish filtering through, then poured them each a mug.

"Have you heard anything about Ben?" she asked, thanking him for the coffee with a weak smile.

Christian told her what he'd learned.

Mariah held the cup tightly with both hands. She was paler than he could remember, and the urge to take her into his arms and comfort her was strong. It hurt to realize she didn't want him.

"How'd you sleep?" he asked, perching on the corner of her desk.

"I didn't."

"Me neither."

"I...don't know if I'm going to get much work done today," she murmured, avoiding his eyes.

The door opened again, and Sawyer entered. He paused when he saw Christian so close to Mariah. Christian started to tell him what he knew about Ben.

"I talked to Bethany myself," Sawyer said, interrupting him. "Charles and Lanni are flying into Fairbanks this morning to be with her. Mitch, too. They'll keep in close touch and let us know about any changes."

"Good," Christian said. But he wished Sawyer hadn't arrived just then, because he wanted—needed—to talk to Mariah.

"I . . . I started to tell Christian I didn't know if I was going to be much help around here," Mariah said, sounding strangely fragile.

"Take the day off," Sawyer suggested. "I wouldn't be here myself if wasn't necessary." He yawned loudly and rubbed a hand over his eyes. "I doubt anyone got any sleep last night. Abbey and I didn't, that's for sure, and the kids were up half the night, too."

"Everyone loves Ben," Christian said.

"The guy makes me mad," Sawyer said angrily. "He should've hired help a long time ago. Running the café alone is too much for him."

Christian had felt the same kind of anger and realized now that it was directed at himself. The symptoms had been there all along. The fatigue, shortness of breath—the very fact he'd hired Mariah. He should have recognized Ben's increasing weakness. His guilt increased tenfold, knowing he'd taken Mariah away from Ben.

Mariah reached for her jacket. "Thank you. I'm sure I'll feel better tomorrow morning. When you find out about Ben's surgery, I'd appreciate hearing."

"I'll make sure word gets to you," Sawyer promised.

"Thanks."

Christian didn't want Mariah to leave, not until he'd talked to her. "I'll walk you to the lodge," he said.

"Walk her to the lodge?" Sawyer repeated. "Trust me, little brother, she knows the way. Besides, I need you here. We're going to be shorthanded as it is."

Christian wanted to groan with frustration, but when he looked at Mariah, he noticed that she seemed relieved. She didn't welcome his company.

FIVE DAYS LATER Christian sat in the Fairbanks Memorial Hospital waiting lounge. He leaned forward, his elbows resting on his knees. Twice he looked at his watch, wondering how much longer it would be before the nurse caring for Ben would let him into the room.

Ben's surgery had taken place within twenty-four hours of his arrival, and the cantankerous stew-burner was said to be wreaking all kinds of havoc with the staff. One nurse had claimed she'd rather care for a roomful of newborns than take another shift with Ben Hamilton.

Christian smiled just thinking about it.

"You can see Mr. Hamilton now."

Christian barely noticed the woman who spoke. He leapt out of his seat before she could change her mind and headed toward Ben's room.

To Christian's surprise, his friend was sitting up in bed, and although he was pale, his coloring was decidedly better than before the surgery. Above all, Ben was alive.

Very much alive.

"Quit looking at me like you're viewing buzzard bait," he grumbled.

Christian burst out laughing. "Damn, but it's good to see you."

"Yeah, well, I don't mind saying it's a pleasure to see you, too." Ben grinned, but the effort appeared to tax him. "From what I understand, if it wasn't for Mariah I wouldn't be here now."

"That's right." Christian pulled a chair close to the bed and sat down.

"Speaking of Mariah," Ben said, dropping his head back against the pillow. "You still denying you're in love with her?"

A week earlier, and Christian would have raised a ruckus denouncing any such thing. What a difference this past week had made. "No," he answered flatly.

"Is she leaving Hard Luck?"

"I don't know what her plans are at this point."

"For heaven's sake, are you going to marry her or not?"

Leave it to Ben to zero in on the one question that remained unanswered in his mind. It had taken him far longer than it should have to recognize the truth about his feelings toward Mariah. In retrospect, he was embarrassed to admit how dense he'd been. He didn't know exactly when he'd come to care for her so deeply—somewhere between the day of her arrival when she'd chased her underwear across the runway and the night she'd saved Ben's life.

Okay, he could admit he loved her, but did that mean he had to *do* something about it?

"I'm not ready for marriage," he declared.

Ben chuckled, the sound pitifully weak. "Have you talked it over with Mariah?"

"No." He hadn't even told her he loved her yet.

"What are you afraid of, son?"

Yeah, Ben always did have a way of getting right to the heart of the matter. "I don't know." It wasn't like he

wanted to play the field; his dates with Vickie and particularly Allison had proved that. He'd gone out with
one of the most beautiful women he'd ever met and
spent the entire night wishing he was with Mariah.

Even Vickie, who at one time had been head-over-
heels crazy about him, was ready to toss him to the
wolves because he'd spent their date talking about Mariah. Other women bored him. He wanted a woman who
was strong and funny and brave and sweet.

A woman like Mariah.

"Seems to me you don't know what you want," Ben
said.

"I do know what I want," Christian responded. "My
problem is I don't know what to do about it." He sat for
several more minutes, thinking. When he looked up
again he found Ben asleep. He stood and gently squeezed
his friend's arm. It was time he headed back to Hard
Luck, anyway.

Ben was going to be just fine.

MARIAH LOVED TO SIT out on the lodge's porch swing.
The late-September afternoon was filled with glorious
sunshine. Colors had started to change and the tundra
was ablaze in orange and reds. Snow would arrive soon;
in fact, there had already been a light snowfall a few
nights ago. Before long the rivers would freeze, and
daylight would be almost nonexistent.

She loved Hard Luck, loved Alaska, and didn't want
to leave. She knew she needed to make a decision, but
had delayed it.

Although Karen and Matt had offered to let her stay
indefinitely at the lodge, Mariah had declined. Their
generosity had touched her heart, but they had enough
to do with the arrival of the baby and operating their

tour business. An extra guest, even a paying one, would be a burden they didn't need.

That meant Mariah had to make a number of important decisions regarding her future.

It also meant she couldn't stay in Hard Luck.

And yet the thought of leaving filled her with unbearable sadness. Hard Luck was her home, more so than Seattle, where she'd been born and raised. Her friends were here.

Christian was here.

Gently moving the swing back and forth, she surveyed her options. She was so deep in thought she didn't hear Christian's approach.

"Mariah?" He stood on the top step and wrapped one arm around the support column.

Although his voice was soft, she nearly leapt off the swing so great was her surprise. It astonished her that he could have made it all the way to the porch without her noticing.

"Do you have a minute?"

He must've known she was desperately searching for a plausible excuse to avoid him because he added, "I talked to Ben this morning."

"How is he?" she asked, eager for news.

"Resting comfortably. He sends his love."

"I'll try to get into Fairbanks this week to visit him myself," she said, realizing she sounded nervous. Well, she was. Being around Christian, especially outside the work environment, had always left her feeling tongue-tied and uneasy.

He moved across the porch and sat next to her on the swing. "I have something I'd like to discuss with you."

Mariah locked her fingers together, vowing to be strong. "I'm not coming back to work for you, Christian—no matter how much of a raise you offer."

"This doesn't have anything to do with the office. This has to do with you and me."

Mariah felt as if the world went still, as if the wind stopped blowing, the sun ceased to shine and the whole world waited in silent suspension for him to continue.

"Us?" Her voice rose to a squeak. Resolutely she closed her mouth. Every time she talked to Christian, she seemed to say something stupid. Like raving about a salmon casserole. Or telling him to shut up because he was disturbing her fantasy. No wonder he sought out more sophisticated companionship. With her he got salmon casserole, she thought wryly; with Allison Reynolds it was T-bone steak.

"Yes, us," he repeated gently. "Actually I'd like to know what your plans are for the winter."

He wanted her gone. That was what this was leading to. He was going to ask her to leave Hard Luck.

She remained silent.

"Matt told me you've decided not to stay at the lodge. That doesn't leave you a lot of options, housing here being what it is."

"No," she admitted, and looked away as the pain burned a hole straight through her. "Let me make this easy for you. You're asking me to leave Hard Luck and I—"

"What?" he demanded, laughing as if what she'd just said was ludicrous.

Mariah didn't take kindly to his humor. She had nowhere to go except back to Seattle. Her parents would soon suffocate her with attention and *their* plans for her future. She felt too defeated, too discouraged, to make a new start in some new place. What hurt so terribly was that the man who held her heart in the palm of his hand was the one asking her to leave.

"I'll go without a fuss," she whispered.

"Mariah." Christian caught her by the shoulders and turned her so that she faced him squarely. "I'm not asking you to leave Hard Luck. Quite the opposite." His gaze pinned hers and she read the truth in his eyes. "I came to ask you to be my wife."

"Your wife?" Something wasn't right. "Is this a joke?" she asked angrily.

"No man makes that kind of offer unless he's serious. And, Mariah, I've never been more serious in my life. I want to marry you."

Probably for the first time since her arrival in Alaska, Mariah was struck dumb.

"Say something," Christian urged.

Her heart melted at the uncertainty in his voice. After all this time, he still didn't know she was crazy in love with him.

"Kiss me," she said when she found the ability to speak.

"Kiss you?" He glanced over his shoulder. "Right here? Now?"

"Yes," she said impatiently.

"This isn't another one of those fantasy things, is it? Because what I feel for you is real."

"This request is very real, too. Now kindly shut up and kiss me."

"Just remember," he whispered as he reached for her, "you asked for this." He brought her into his arms and slowly, methodically, lowered his mouth to hers.

In the beginning his kiss was gentle and tender, the way it had been the night of the dance. Soon he increased the pressure, parting her lips with the tip of his tongue. Mariah moaned softly, clinging fiercely to his arms. They quickly discovered that one kiss wasn't enough to satisfy either of them. They kissed again and again.

A sensation of weightlessness stole over her. She felt as if she could fly, float effortlessly through the bright, clear sky. Already her heart was soaring.

"Soon," Christian whispered, breaking off the kiss and burying his face in the curve of her neck.

"Soon?" she repeated, confused.

"We're getting married very soon."

"But—"

"I don't know any man who could have behaved more like a fool than I have toward you this past year: I love you, Mariah, heart and soul. I need you in my life."

Mariah brushed the tears from her face. "You're . . . sure about all this?" Loving him the way she did, she couldn't bear it if he suddenly changed his mind.

"Oh, yes," he said, and kissed her again. "*Will* you marry me, Mariah?"

Smiling through her tears, she nodded eagerly.

Christian threw back his head and laughed.

"That wasn't supposed to be funny, Christian O'Halloran!"

"Not you, my love," he said, wrapping her more securely in his arms. "Us."

"*Us* is humorous?" If she wasn't so elated, so filled with joy, she could take offense at this.

"We're going to be very happy, Mariah." He kissed her once more in a way that left no doubt as to his feelings. "I've waited all my life for you."

"Christian! I swear you're the most obtuse man in the entire state of Alaska."

"I couldn't agree with you more," he admitted, his eyes holding hers. "It took me a while to figure things out, but I fully intend to make up for lost time."

Mariah laid her head on his shoulder and nestled into his embrace. "And I fully intend to let you."

"I meant what I said, Mariah. I want us to be married as soon as we can make the arrangements." He looked down at her as if he anticipated an argument, but Mariah didn't have any objections.

Not a single, solitary one.

* * * * *

Now that Christian, the last O'Halloran brother, has succumbed to love, what about his friend Duke? If opposites really do attract, is there a chance that Duke Porter—top Midnight Sons pilot and a real "man's man"—can find happiness with Tracy Santiago—lawyer, city woman and outspoken feminist? Find out in Debbie Macomber's final Midnight Sons *story, ENDING IN MARRIAGE.*
Available next month.

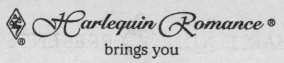
Harlequin Romance ®

brings you

How the West Was Wooed!

We've rounded up twelve of our most popular authors, and the result is a whole year of romance, Western style. Every month we'll be bringing you a spirited, independent woman whose heart is about to be lassoed by a rugged, handsome, one-hundred-percent cowboy! Watch for...

- April: **A DANGEROUS MAGIC**—Patricia Wilson

- May: **THE BADLANDS BRIDE**—Rebecca Winters

- June: **RUNAWAY WEDDING**—Ruth Jean Dale

- July: **A RANCH, A RING AND EVERYTHING**—Val Daniels

- August: **TEMPORARY TEXAN**—Heather Allison

HITCH-3

HARLEQUIN PRESENTS®

Harlequin brings you the best books by the best authors!

ROBYN DONALD

"...features enticing characters guaranteed to knock your socks off." —*Romantic Times*

&

DIANA HAMILTON

"...shows her skills to perfection."
—*Affaire de Coeur*

Coming next month:

Element of Risk by Robyn Donald
Harlequin Presents #1803

Hostage of Passion by Diana Hamilton
Harlequin Presents #1804

Harlequin Presents—the best has just gotten better!
Available in April wherever Harlequin books are sold.

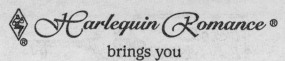

Harlequin Romance®

brings you

Some men are worth waiting for!

They're handsome, they're charming but, best of all, they're single! Twelve lucky women are about to discover that finding Mr. Right is not a problem—it's holding on to him.

In April the series continues with

#3406 THE RIGHT KIND OF MAN
by Jessica Hart

Skye had run away from man trouble, only to bump smack into Lorimer Kingan. He was tall, dark and handsome, and he wanted an efficient, reliable PA. Skye desperately wanted the job, but could she really describe herself as *efficient*? Worse, she knew as soon as she saw him that Lorimer was the right kind of man for her!

Hold out for Harlequin Romance's heroes in coming months...

- May: MOVING IN WITH ADAM—Jeanne Allan
- June: THE DADDY TRAP—Leigh Michaels
- July: THE BACHELOR'S WEDDING—Betty Neels

BRIDE'S BAY RESORT

UNLOCK THE DOOR TO GREAT ROMANCE AT BRIDE'S BAY RESORT

Join Harlequin's new across-the-lines series, set in an exclusive hotel on an island off the coast of South Carolina.

Seven of your favorite authors will bring you exciting stories about fascinating heroes and heroines discovering love at Bride's Bay Resort.

Look for these fabulous stories coming to a store near you beginning in January 1996.

Harlequin American Romance #613 in January
Matchmaking Baby by Cathy Gillen Thacker

Harlequin Presents #1794 in February
Indiscretions by Robyn Donald

Harlequin Intrigue #362 in March
Love and Lies by Dawn Stewardson

Harlequin Romance #3404 in April
Make Believe Engagement by Day Leclaire

Harlequin Temptation #588 in May
Stranger in the Night by Roseanne Williams

Harlequin Superromance #695 in June
Married to a Stranger by Connie Bennett

Harlequin Historicals #324 in July
Dulcie's Gift by Ruth Langan

Visit Bride's Bay Resort each month wherever Harlequin books are sold.

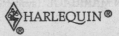

HARLEQUIN ®

BBAYG

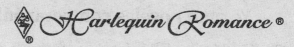

Harlequin Romance ®

New from Harlequin Romance
a very special six-book series by

MIDNIGHT SONS

DEBBIE MACOMBER

The town of Hard Luck, Alaska, needs women!

The O'Halloran brothers, who run a bush-plane service
called **Midnight Sons**, are heading a campaign to
attract women to Hard Luck. *(Location: north of the
Arctic Circle. Population: 150—mostly men!)*

"Debbie Macomber's *Midnight Sons* series is a delightful
romantic saga. And each book is a powerful, engaging story
in its own right. Unforgettable!"

—Linda Lael Miller

TITLE IN THE MIDNIGHT SONS SERIES:

Yo amo novelas con corazón!

Starting this March, Harlequin opens up to a whole new world of readers with two new romance lines in SPANISH!

Harlequin Deseo
- passionate, sensual and exciting stories

Harlequin Bianca
- romances that are fun, fresh and very contemporary

With four titles a month, each line will offer the same wonderfully romantic stories that you've come to love—now available in Spanish.

Look for them at selected retail outlets.

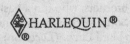 HARLEQUIN®

HARLEQUIN PRESENTS

HARLEQUIN PRESENTS
men you won't be able to resist falling in love with...

HARLEQUIN PRESENTS
women who have feelings just like your own...

HARLEQUIN PRESENTS
powerful passion in exotic international settings...

HARLEQUIN PRESENTS
intense, dramatic stories that will keep you turning
to the very last page...

HARLEQUIN PRESENTS
The world's bestselling romance series!